Civil Liberties

Bethany Christian
High School Library
Goshen, Indiana

Look for these and other books in the Lucent Overview Series:

Abortion	Health Care
Acid Rain	The Holocaust
Adoption	Homeless Children
Advertising	Homelessness
Alcoholism	Illegal Immigration
Animal Rights	Illiteracy
Artificial Organs	Immigration
The Brain	Juvenile Crime
Cancer	Memory
Censorship	Mental Illness
Child Abuse	Militias
Children's Rights	Money
Cities	Ocean Pollution
Civil Liberties	Oil Spills
Cloning	The Olympic Games
Cults	Organ Transplants
Dealing with Death	Ozone
Death Penalty	Paranormal Phenomena
Democracy	Pesticides
Drug Abuse	Police Brutality
Drugs and Sports	Population
Drug Trafficking	Poverty
Eating Disorders	Prisons
Elections	Rainforests
Endangered Species	The Rebuilding of Bosnia
The End of Apartheid in South Africa	Recycling
Energy Alternatives	The Reunification of Germany
Epidemics	Schools
Espionage	Smoking
Ethnic Violence	Space Exploration
Euthanasia	Sports in America
Extraterrestrial Life	Suicide
Family Violence	The UFO Challenge
Gangs	The United Nations
Garbage	The U.S. Congress
Gay Rights	The U.S. Presidency
Genetic Engineering	Vanishing Wetlands
The Greenhouse Effect	Vietnam
Gun Control	Women's Rights
Hate Groups	World Hunger
Hazardous Waste	Zoos

Civil Liberties

by Debbie Levy

Library of Congress Cataloging-in-Publication Data

Levy, Debbie.
    Civil liberties / by Debbie Levy.
       p. cm. — (Lucent overview series)
    Includes bibliographical references and index.
    Summary: Discusses civil liberties guaranteed by the Constitution including freedom of speech and assembly, media freedoms, religious liberties, and right to privacy.
    ISBN 1-56006-611-3   (lib. bdg. : alk. paper)
    1. Civil rights—United States—Juvenile literature.   [1. Civil rights.]   I. Title.   II. Series.
KF4750.L48   2000
342.73'085—dc21   99-33792
                                                                              CIP

No part of this book may be reproduced or used in any form or by any means, electrical, mechanical, or otherwise, including, but not limited to, photocopy, recording, or any information storage and retrieval system, without prior written permission from the publisher.

Copyright © 2000 by Lucent Books, Inc.
P.O. Box 289011, San Diego, CA 92198-9011
Printed in the U.S.A.

Contents

INTRODUCTION	6
CHAPTER ONE The Scope of Civil Liberties	10
CHAPTER TWO Freedom of Speech and Assembly	20
CHAPTER THREE Media Freedoms	37
CHAPTER FOUR Religious Liberties	52
CHAPTER FIVE The Right to Privacy	67
NOTES	85
ORGANIZATIONS TO CONTACT	90
SUGGESTIONS FOR FURTHER READING	95
WORKS CONSULTED	97
INDEX	105
PICTURE CREDITS	111
ABOUT THE AUTHOR	112

Introduction

Sweet land of liberty.... With liberty and justice for all.... Give me liberty, or give me death!

PHRASES ECHOING THE theme of liberty run through American history and culture as surely as a river runs toward the sea. Americans cherish liberty, and the United States was founded on the understanding that people are entitled to it.

To promote the common good, however, America's national, state, and local governments may adopt laws and rules that curtail freedom. These legal limitations generally reflect the wishes of the majority of the citizens, who elect representatives to govern the country. Everyone must follow the limits set by the majority-elected government, even people who disagree with them. Those who think they should be free to use illegal drugs, for example, will still be arrested if police find drugs in their possession. People who want to drive sixty-five miles per hour down a thirty-five-mph street will still have to face the consequences, if stopped by police.

However, there are some rules the majority may not impose. Some freedoms are protected from governmental interference regardless of how many citizens want to limit them. These are called civil liberties. Civil liberties are the freedoms that individuals are guaranteed to possess despite any laws or regulations the government might try to impose.

The very first words of the U.S. Constitution refer to these liberties: "We the people of the United States, in Order to form a more perfect Union, establish Justice ... *and secure the Blessings of Liberty to ourselves and our Posterity*, do ordain and establish this Constitution for the United States of America." Ironically, despite this express resolve to protect "the Blessings of Liberty," nothing in the main text of the Constitution explicitly addresses civil liberties at all.

The Bill of Rights

The men who wrote the Constitution in 1787 were more concerned with crafting a strong national government for the young country than with specifying individual liberties. The Constitution that went into effect the following year did not include a bill of rights or any other list of civil liberties guaranteed to individual citizens.

However, many influential citizens feared the power of a strong government. Such fears were based on experience. Citizens in the new nation had recent memories of occasions when governments had stifled freedom by punishing people for their religious beliefs, for example, or for expressing their opinions publicly. Thus several states included a "bill of rights" in their own constitutions, which they adopted after the American Revolution.

Although the Constitution refers to the protection of liberty, its founders were more concerned with crafting a strong national government.

In 1789, James Madison proposed nine amendments for the U.S. Congress to consider adding to the text of the Constitution. After debate, alteration, and additions, the House of Representatives and Senate voted to add twelve amendments to the Constitution and sent them to the states for the necessary approval. By 1791, the states had adopted ten of the amendments, which today are known as the Bill of Rights. It is through the Bill of Rights that the Constitution limits the government's powers over individual liberty.

New challenges

Disputes over civil liberties today reflect the same issues that concerned lawmakers two hundred years ago. Controversies over newspaper articles, political demonstrations, and religious discrimination, for example, continue to arise and to be settled by application of the principles contained in the Bill of Rights.

New ideas and technology have raised new questions about civil liberties. For example, recent governmental efforts to limit sexually explicit materials on the Internet have been met with challenges and lawsuits based on the Bill of Rights' guarantee of freedom of speech. As another example, law enforcement authorities across the country sometimes allow news reporters and film crews to ride along with police to record their activities. The resulting newspaper or television coverage can be quite dramatic and informative, serving the interests of both the media and the police. But some of the people caught on film while the police searched their homes have sued the government for violating their right to privacy.

Courts and legislators have reached varying conclusions in controversies involving the Internet and police "ride-alongs" as to whether these governmental actions actually infringed constitutional liberties. But these conclusions have not varied in one important respect: The Bill of Rights is flexible enough to apply to situations that the authors of those rights could never have foreseen.

Still, over the years, Americans have wished that the nation's founders had been more specific on the subject of lib-

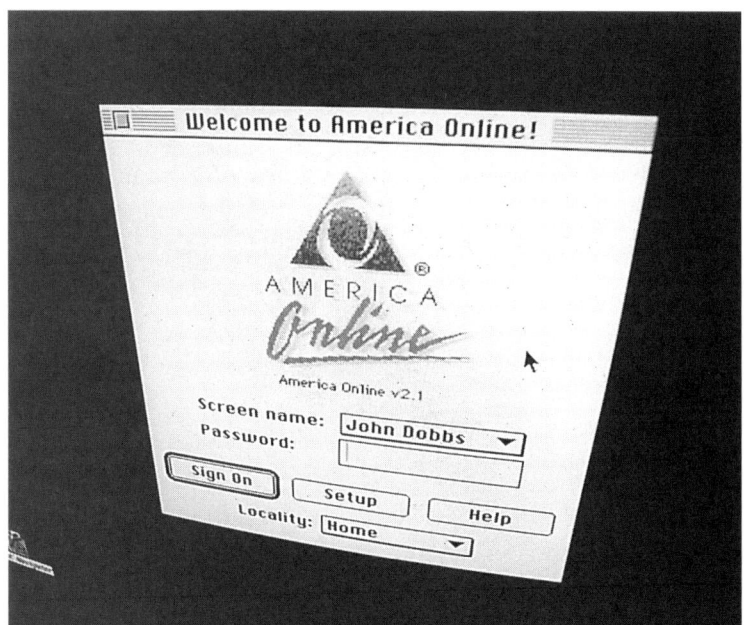

The Internet has given rise to new challenges and lawsuits based on civil liberties claims.

erty. In a speech made in Baltimore in 1864, President Abraham Lincoln said, "The world has never had a good definition of the word liberty, and the American people, just now, are much in want of one." Interestingly, it may be the very lack of specificity about the meaning of liberty that has made the Constitution and Bill of Rights so durable and versatile in the face of change. Indeed, Lincoln himself offered not a precise definition, but rather a homespun approach to understanding liberty: "The shepherd drives the wolf from the sheep's throat, for which the sheep thanks the shepherd as a *liberator*, while the wolf denounces him for the same act as the destroyer of liberty."[1]

Many thousands of words have been expended on the subject of civil liberties. Those words reflect how dearly individual freedom is held in the hearts of Americans and how suspiciously governmental action that appears to limit liberty is viewed. President Lincoln's observation—that one person's (or sheep's) liberty may be another's burden—highlights the challenge of America's democracy, as well as that of civil liberties: The majority may rule, but individual freedom must also reign.

1

The Scope of Civil Liberties

NO SINGLE DOCUMENT could possibly specify all the circumstances in which individual freedom might need protection from governmental action. The Constitution (including the Bill of Rights) deals in broad categories, which courts apply to particular conflicts and claims. Among the leading liberties guaranteed by the Bill of Rights are freedom of speech and assembly, freedom of the press, and freedom of religion, including both a right to exercise one's religion freely and a ban on any governmental "establishment" of religion. Also guaranteed are the rights of individuals to be secure against "unreasonable searches and seizures" and to enjoy "due process of law" before being deprived of "life, liberty, or property."

The freedoms written down in the Bill of Rights do not necessarily mark the full extent of Americans' liberties. Other rights, not mentioned in the Constitution or Bill of Rights, have come to be considered civil liberties that the government may not violate. Chief among these unwritten (or unenumerated) civil liberties is privacy—what U.S. Supreme Court Justice Louis D. Brandeis called "the right to be left alone."[2] Among other things, the right to privacy includes the (limited) right to choose an abortion, to use birth control, and to refuse medical intervention for non-contagious illness.

The Bill of Rights explicitly protects individual liberties from infringement by the federal government. The First

Amendment, for example, admonishes that "Congress shall make no law" prohibiting the free exercise of religion, abridging freedom of speech, and so on. By its terms, the Bill of Rights seems not to apply to the states. So, are states and their subdivisions—counties, cities, towns—free to ignore the civil liberties guaranteed in the Bill of Rights? Could Alabama, for example, adopt a law or a state constitutional provision that made burning a flag to protest governmental policy a crime, even though such protest is considered protected expression under the First Amendment? Could New York City ban marches by groups who preach hate toward Jews or African-Americans, even though federal judges have ruled that people enjoy the right under the First Amendment to attempt even to spread hatred through offensive words, signs, and pamphlets?

The answer is no. After the Civil War the states adopted the Thirteenth, Fourteenth, and Fifteenth Amendments to the Constitution, which expressly extended protection to

Although many people believe flag burning should be a crime, the First Amendment protects such conduct under its guarantee of freedom of expression.

individuals from various actions by the states. The Thirteenth Amendment outlawed slavery. The Fifteenth Amendment made race an impermissible basis on which to deny a citizen the right to vote.

But it is the Fourteenth Amendment—"No State shall ... deprive any person of life, liberty, or property, without due process of law"—that is the key to civil liberties in the states. The Supreme Court has interpreted this to mean that state governments must observe and protect the fundamental individual liberties in the Bill of Rights just as the federal government must.

A common thread

At first glance, the written and unwritten liberties protected by the Bill of Rights and the Fourteenth Amendment may seem a haphazard assortment. In fact, they are unified by a common thread. That thread is the notion that some human activities should be off-limits to governmental interference. These activities—political speech and protest, for example—may be protected because they are essential to a properly working representative government. Or, the activities—choices about reproduction or medical treatment, for example—may concern intimate matters that society believes are best placed beyond governmental control. Alternatively, liberties may be protected because they are fundamental to individual human fulfillment or dignity, such as religious practices and nonpolitical expression.

Another strand in the thread that is common to civil liberties is that they all concern freedoms from governmental action, rather than freedom from individual responsibility. In other words, Americans have the right to be free from governmental regulation of speech; the press has the right to be free from governmental encroachment; the government must not establish an official religion. But if, for example, a person is hired by a restaurant to perform the job of greeting patrons pleasantly at the front door, he cannot argue that his "free speech" rights have been violated when the restaurant fires him for greeting people with critical comments about their appearance.

Such racist groups as the Ku Klux Klan are free to voice their opinions even though they are in direct conflict with others.

Still, civil liberties do involve relationships and conflicts among individuals or groups. Usually this happens when one group has succeeded in gaining governmental action favorable to its interests. For example, in some communities citizens have convinced officials to require public libraries to use "blocking software" that bars users of a library's computers from accessing sexually explicit or violent Internet material. Others in those same communities have invoked the First Amendment's guarantee of freedom of speech to try to dissuade the local government from limiting Internet accessibility this way. In Loudon County, Virginia, although such an appeal to free speech concerns did not change the Loudon Library Board's mind in 1998, it did convince a federal judge to overturn the board's computer blocking rule, in the first court case of its kind. The judge in that case, a former librarian, ruled that the library board's policy "offends the guarantee of free speech in the First Amendment" and was contrary to the goal of "offering the widest possible diversity of views and expressions."[3]

Guardians of liberties

When civil liberties are at issue, various groups and individuals may come forward or be called upon to protect those freedoms. Diverse organizations such as the American Civil Liberties Union (ACLU), People for the American Way, the Institute for Justice, the Rutherford Institute, and many others have taken upon themselves the task of building public support for their view of civil liberties and advocating for laws and court rulings favorable to their views. The ACLU, for example, participated in the 1970s court cases that overturned criminal laws against abortion, and today the ACLU is at the forefront of opposition to what it considers governmental interference in religious matters. In contrast, in 1998, the Institute for Justice, which describes itself as a "principled alternative" to the ACLU, helped families in Milwaukee convince the Wisconsin Supreme Court to uphold a law allowing low-income children the use of state funds to pay for tuition to attend church-supported schools.

Such interest groups, while they may influence the outcome in a conflict over civil liberties, do not determine the final result. Lawmakers—at the local, state, and national levels—have the power to adopt legislation that protects civil liberties, or at least laws that implement the majority's view of civil liberties. For example, many states have adopted "two-party consent" laws, which outlaw the taping of private telephone conversations without both the caller's and the recipient's consent. Among the laws passed by Congress to safeguard civil liberties are the Privacy Act of 1974 (preventing federal agencies from the misuse of personal data) and the Equal Access Act of 1984 (requiring public schools to grant the same access to religious student clubs as they give to nonreligious ones).

Legislators, however, also do not have the final say on civil liberties. Ultimately, the courts decide the scope and content of civil liberties, whether those liberties are defined by the Constitution, Congress, or state and local legislatures. Final decisions on questions of constitutional freedoms are made by the highest court in the land, the U.S. Supreme Court. The nine Supreme Court justices make their rulings by a majority vote and usually explain their decisions in written opinions. However, the Supreme Court does not have the time or resources to consider every civil liberties dispute that arises. Accordingly, the lower federal courts (trial courts, known as federal district courts, and appeals courts, called federal circuit courts) and hundreds of state courts across the country are also essential guardians of civil liberties.

Even a Supreme Court decision is not necessarily the last word on a civil liberties question. From time to time, the Court has revised and reinterpreted the scope of civil liberties—particularly free speech and protest, as well as privacy—as Americans' ideas about freedom have evolved and as new Supreme Court justices with different ideas about civil liberties have been appointed. Often the interpretations evolve gradually, but they may also shift abruptly, as was the case when the Supreme Court first upheld mandatory flag salute laws in 1940 and then declared them a violation of the First Amendment in 1943.

The Supreme Court periodically revises and reinterprets civil liberties as new ideas evolve.

Liberties at risk or risky liberties?

Many advocates of civil liberties insist that freedom needs constant, vigilant protection. "In every era of American history," warns the American Civil Liberties Union in a briefing paper, "the government has tried to expand its authority at the expense of individual rights."[4]

Others, who also describe themselves as defenders of liberty, voice a different concern: that the concept of freedom held by many Americans has expanded well beyond what contributes to a productive, orderly, democratic society. Some of these people favor a greater awareness of the individual responsibilities that go hand in hand with individual rights. "The American moral and legal tradition has always acknowledged the need to balance individual rights with the need to protect the safety and health of the public," states the platform of the Communitarian Network. On the question of government searches that may compromise individual privacy, for example, this diverse network of professors, lawyers, business executives, and community activists continues:

> We differ with the ACLU and other radical libertarians who oppose sobriety checkpoints, screening gates at airports, drug and alcohol testing for people who directly affect public safety.... Given the minimal intrusion involved (an average sobriety checkpoint lasts ninety seconds) [and] the importance of the interests at stake (we have lost more lives, many due to drunken drivers, on the road each year than in the war in Vietnam) ... these and similar reasonable measures should receive full public support.[5]

Liberties in conflict

In theory, civil liberties are hard to argue against. In practice, however, controversies brew when freedoms and rights collide with each other. As the saying goes, "Your right to swing your fist ends at the tip of my nose." Many complex and difficult cases involve high stakes and principles, conflicting concepts of right versus right. The situations in which these conflicts arise are as varied as human activity.

Battles have erupted across the country, for example, over demonstrations at abortion clinics. Under the Constitution's free speech guarantees, antiabortion activists enjoy the right to march and picket to express their opposition to abortion. On the other hand, the U.S. Supreme Court has ruled that a pregnant woman is guaranteed the liberty to obtain an abortion. When antiabortion demonstrators are most vigorous and effective outside a clinic that provides abortion services, they may interfere with the right of access of patients to the clinic.

One way to deal with such clashes of interest is to compromise: In 1994, the Supreme Court ruled that a thirty-six-foot

Some vigorous antiabortion demonstrators interfere with a patient's right to obtain an abortion.

no-protest zone around a Florida abortion clinic was permissible but that the law could not stop protesters from approaching patients within three hundred feet of the clinic. In this case, protesters got some of what they wanted, which was acknowledgment of their right to protest near a clinic; abortion providers and patients won acknowledgment of their right to be protected from interference.

Some believe that compromising on civil liberties is not appropriate, however. In 1998, when officials in Casper, Wyoming, adopted a fifty-foot no-protest zone around the church funeral of a gay murder victim, they said their goal was to protect public safety and "the . . . rights of not only those protesting, but those wanting to go into the church."[6] However, argued Jay Sekulow, chief counsel of the American Center for Law and Justice, there is no "funeral exception" to the freedom of speech; a desire to be sensitive to mourners may not impinge on the free speech rights of antigay activists, not even for fifty feet.

Questionable compromises

As Sekulow's objection suggests, compromise in cases of conflicting liberties might be viewed by some as an unacceptable whittling away of a right that is supposed to be fundamental. Nowhere is this dilemma more sharply presented than in the controversy over religion in public schools, which has become a perennial feature in American public policy debates.

The U.S. Supreme Court outlawed mandatory school prayer in 1962 and mandatory Bible reading in school in 1963, explaining in both cases that those practices violate the First Amendment's "Establishment Clause," which bans any government establishment of religion. Denying religious practices presented difficulties, the justices acknowledged, because the First Amendment also guarantees an individual's right to free exercise of his or her religion—even in school. Today many religious groups echo what President Bill Clinton observed in a 1995 memorandum, that "some school officials, teachers and parents have assumed that religious expression of any type is either inappropriate or forbidden altogether in public schools." In that same memorandum, Clinton voiced his view that "nothing in the First Amendment converts our public schools into religion-free zones, or requires all religious expression to be left behind at the schoolhouse door."[7]

Problems arise, however, when school officials and communities attempt to craft compromises to achieve a balance between the Establishment Clause and the Free Exercise Clause. In Pontotoc County, Mississippi, for example, the public schools—reflecting the wishes of a majority of the community—broadcast devotionals over the public address system and conducted Bible study classes. To address complaints by one family that this practice violated the Establishment Clause, a teacher put headphones over the ears of seven-year-old Jason Herdahl so that he did not have to hear the morning prayers.

Jason's mother sued and presented evidence that all five of the Herdahl children had been taunted by other children, particularly after implementation of the headphone compromise. In 1996 U.S. District Court Judge Neal B. Biggers Jr. ruled that the school's practices violated the First Amendment. "The Bill of Rights was created to protect the minority from tyranny of the majority,"[8] Judge Biggers said. In this judge's view, the compromise of excusing children from participating in the school's religious program could not save the program, since the compromise still led to an impermissible establishment of religion.

When liberties collide, whether with other liberties or other interests, the resulting dispute presents difficult choices. The history of civil liberties is a chronicle of similar dilemmas. The progress of civil liberties in the United States can be seen not so much as a saga in which citizens have fought a government intent on crushing individual freedom, but rather as a series of conflicts in which one group's rights (to pray, to demonstrate) impinge on another group's rights (to be free from coerced religion, to obtain an abortion). In a nation with increasingly competing interests, the future of civil liberties promises to continue this pattern.

2

Freedom of Speech and Assembly

"CONGRESS SHALL MAKE no law... abridging the freedom of speech." These words in the First Amendment to the Constitution are at issue when the government seeks to limit individual expression, whether that expression takes the form of words (political advocacy, racial slurs, song lyrics) or expressive conduct (wearing a peace symbol or swastika, burning a cross, trampling an American flag). The paradox that often underlies free speech conflicts is that the more the majority may object to certain speech, the more that speech may require, and even deserve, First Amendment protection. At the same time, the more protection given to words and actions under the First Amendment, the more society may be exposed to potential harm and risky choices.

The marketplace of ideas

Some wonder why speech, particularly speech that most people find objectionable and that may promote harmful consequences, is protected. The most famous defense of free speech was made by Supreme Court Justice Oliver Wendell Holmes. "[T]he best test of truth," he wrote, "is in the power of the thought to get itself accepted in the competition of the market."[9] In other words, when people are free to discuss even offensive ideas in an atmosphere of robust debate, the truth that emerges will have the greatest possible authority, precisely because it is allowed to emerge in the face of opposing ideas. This argument is often made by those who defend the rights of groups such as the Ku Klux Klan to hold rallies promoting racism and religious intolerance. "When the voices of hate and intolerance grow louder," explain authors Ellen Alderman and Caroline Kennedy, "when the Klan holds rallies in Georgia and skinheads camp out in California, the most effective rebuttal, in this view, is to see them outnumbered by those who abhor racism and believe in peaceful pluralism."[10]

Another argument in support of a permissive approach to offensive speech is that, as Justice Holmes further noted, "time has upset many fighting faiths."[11] In this view, what seems absolutely true today may turn out to be false tomorrow, and vice versa. American history provides poignant examples of this idea, as well as futile efforts to suppress speech challenging the established wisdom. For example, once it was considered by some to be "true" that human beings had a right to own other human beings as slaves.

Groups, such as these neo-Nazis, are free to discuss offensive ideas like violence and supremacy.

A criminal law in pre–Civil War Virginia punished anyone who denied "by speaking or writing . . . that owners have no right of property in slaves."[12] A few years later, of course, it was no longer "true" that people could own other people.

The marketplace theory of free speech holds that the best response to speech that seems inappropriate is more speech, not suppression. Rather than suppress an idea on the grounds that it is wrong or objectionable, the marketplace model says that offensive speech should be combated through the expression of opposing views.

Not everyone agrees that the marketplace model is appropriate in every situation. In some circumstances society may not enjoy the luxury of time to wait for the truth to prevail over dangerous falsehoods. For example, when those who are spreading falsehoods make use of the mass media, there is a concern that speech that will counter those falsehoods will never be heard. A related argument is that hateful speech that denies the right of other groups to exist or speak should not benefit from First Amendment protection. Reflecting this view, Yale Law School professor Owen Fiss has argued that hate speech and pornography by their very nature are likely to overwhelm and silence other speech and therefore may be restricted by the government.

To date, the rulings of the U.S. Supreme Court tend to reflect the marketplace view of the First Amendment—although often with exceptions, restrictions, and distinctions that can be as confusing as they are important. It is around those confusing fault lines in the Court's interpretation of the First Amendment's free speech structure that most significant controversies over freedom of expression develop.

Dangerous words

Perhaps the most evident fault line is the conflict between the First Amendment's promise of free speech and the fear of violence that might result from speech that incites people to act dangerously. One of the main purposes of government is to preserve a peaceful society, yet speech that advocates violence or dangerous action surely thwarts that goal. Is such speech nonetheless protected by the First Amendment?

The short answer is: maybe. The right to free speech is not absolute. In a well-known opinion he wrote for the Supreme Court in 1919, Justice Oliver Wendell Holmes explained that "free speech would not protect a man in falsely shouting 'fire' in a theatre, and causing a panic." But the difficult issue is how to strike a balance—how to accommodate the interests of a peaceful society and freedom of speech. In that same 1919 case, the Supreme Court formulated the famous "clear and present danger" doctrine as a guide. The government may restrict speech, Justice Holmes said, if "the words used are used in such circumstances and are of such a nature as to create a clear and present danger that they will bring about [harmful consequences]."[13]

Dangers of freedom

Over the years the Supreme Court has developed other formulas in its efforts to balance the freedom and the dangers of speech. In *Chaplinsky v. New Hampshire* (1942), the Court held that "insulting or 'fighting words' . . . which by their very utterance inflict injury or tend to incite an immediate breach of the peace," were not protected. Such words, the Court determined, were of "slight social value as a step to truth."[14] In the 1969 case of *Brandenberg v. Ohio*, the Supreme Court reworded the clear and present danger test to strike down the conviction of a member of the Ku Klux Klan. An Ohio law made it a crime for a person to advocate violence as a means of accomplishing political change. But the First Amendment protects the right of people to advocate the use of force, the Court said, unless the advocacy "is directed to inciting or producing imminent lawless action, and is likely to incite or produce such action."[15]

The difficult distinction between truly dangerous speech, which may be suppressed or punished, and speech that may be frightening but is not subject to government restriction was at issue in a highly publicized lawsuit in 1999 involving an antiabortion Internet site. Beneath pictures of fetuses and dripping blood, the website, titled

"The Nuremberg Files," contained a listing of hundreds of doctors and other abortion providers. Some of the listings included the doctors' addresses, names of family members, license plate numbers, photographs, and personal information. The site described the doctors as "baby butchers" and said that abortion foes should stalk them. The names of those doctors who had been murdered had lines drawn through them; those who had been wounded were shaded in gray. Five of the listed doctors, along with Planned Parenthood and the Portland Feminist Women's Health Center, sued the individuals and organizations responsible for the Nuremberg Files site.

In *Planned Parenthood v. American Coalition of Life Activists,* the doctors claimed that the website amounted to an illegal threat because it implicitly encouraged people to harm them. In a climate of growing violence against abortion clinics across the country, they argued, the website amounted to a type of "hit list." Sandi Hansen, executive director of the Oregon chapter of the National Abortion and Reproductive Rights Action League, told the *Washington Post*, "Certainly the strongly implied message here is to go after these doctors by any means necessary. This site should have a responsibility not to yell 'fire' in a crowded movie theater. What they're doing goes beyond free speech. It's a form of terrorism."[16]

Harsh opinions

The Nuremberg Files' creator, antiabortion activist Neal Horsley, said the purpose of the site was not to encourage murder or violence, but to gather information that would be used for political protests against abortion and as evidence in the event abortion is one day outlawed and abortion doctors brought to justice. At the start of the trial, defense attorney Christopher Ferrea told the jury: "This is a case about the threat to kill or injure, which is simply not there. Opinions? Yes, sometimes harsh. But no violence."[17]

The federal judge presiding over the trial seemed to disagree. He instructed the jury that the individuals maintaining the website could be held accountable if they reasonably should have foreseen that the speech would place an average person in fear. Applying this standard, the jury sided with the doctors and awarded them $107 million in damages. Advocates of abortion rights praised the decision. The defendants and some free-speech advocates said the ruling was vulnerable to reversal because, under the Supreme Court formula in *Brandenberg v. Ohio*, only speech that threatens "imminent lawless action" may be punished. First Amendment expert Paul McMasters summarized the problem in a column analyzing the *Planned Parenthood v. American Coalition of Life Activists* case: "Few of us would want to see speech that puts people in fear of their lives go unchallenged. Few of us would want to see freedom of speech restricted."[18] Yet, as in this case and other hard cases, one of those values—freedom from fear or freedom of speech—must bend.

Tough talk makes tough cases

Closely related to speech that advocates violence is hate speech—expression that promotes abuse and ridicule of targeted groups. Purveyors of hate speech verbally attack victims based on their race, sexual orientation, religion, or nationality. They may also use symbolic expression, such as displaying swastikas or burning crosses. Like speech that incites dangerous action, hate speech can be seen as a threat to a peaceful society and perhaps undeserving of First Amendment protection.

At times the Supreme Court has indicated that hate speech is not protected by the First Amendment. The Supreme Court's more recent rulings, however, reflect the proposition that the First Amendment is highly tolerant even of intolerant speech, including racist and bigoted expression. This does not mean that individuals are free to fling racial epithets in the workplace without consequence. Nor may they spray paint Nazi swastikas on synagogues or burn crosses on another family's front lawn. People, organizations, and employers may forbid offensive speech or demonstrations in their own buildings or on their own property. Those who violate private property through hate speech may be subject to criminal prosecution under trespass, harassment, and other laws. They may also be held accountable for damages in a civil lawsuit.

In contrast, speech of any kind—including hate speech—enjoys considerable protection in streets, parks, and public places. These are known as "public forums" in legal parlance. Given their historical significance as cen-

Hate speech, such as this antigay demonstration, is protected in streets, parks, and public places.

Media coverage of the Nazi press conference held at the Nazi Headquarters in Illinois.

ters for debate and demonstration on matters of public interest, public forums are treated as special havens for speech and expressive conduct.

Thus in a landmark ruling in 1978, a federal court held that when the Village of Skokie, Illinois, refused to issue a permit to Nazis to parade in front of the village hall, it violated the First Amendment. Skokie was home to thousands of survivors of the Nazi Holocaust, many of whom objected strenuously to the Nazi presence in their town. The court ruled that because the town's refusal was not motivated by a fear of imminent violence likely to result from the demonstration, but rather was based on the content of the Nazis' message, it violated the Nazis' free speech rights when it denied the parade permit. Similarly, in a different case decided in 1992, the Supreme Court said that a St. Paul, Minnesota, city ordinance that prohibited cross burnings based on their racist and anti-Semitic symbolism was a First Amendment breach.

Despite the wide latitude the Supreme Court and other judges have given hate speech, many find the notion of cloaking such expression in the protections of the First Amendment abhorrent. In a 1997 poll sponsored by the Freedom Forum and conducted by University of Connecticut professor Kenneth Dautrich, 75 percent of the 1,026 people queried said they would not allow people to say things in public that might offend a racial group.

When actions speak louder than words

The Supreme Court has ruled that symbolic expression, whether exhibiting swastikas, burning crosses, or wearing peace signs, is protected by the First Amendment because it is "closely akin to 'pure speech.'"[19] That phrase comes from a 1969 decision, *Tinker v. Des Moines Independent Community School District*, in which the Court held that public school students could wear black armbands in school to protest the Vietnam War. In another controversial ruling in 1989, the Court upheld the right of an individual to burn the American flag in public as a symbolic expression of disagreement with governmental policies. These rulings, like free speech principles generally, apply to expressive conduct carried out on public, not private, property.

In the flag-burning case, a demonstrator at the 1984 Republican National Convention in Dallas destroyed the flag in front of City Hall while others chanted, "America, the red, white, and blue, we spit on you!"[20] Texas law at the time made it a crime to "desecrate" the flag in a way that "the actor knows will seriously offend" onlookers. In reversing the demonstrator's conviction under this law, the Supreme Court said, "If there is a bedrock principle underlying the First Amendment, it is that the Government may not prohibit the expression of an idea simply because society finds the idea itself offensive or disagreeable."[21]

In response to the decision in this case, *Texas v. Johnson*, Congress passed the Flag Protection Act of 1989, which punished anyone who "knowingly mutilates, defaces, physically defiles, burns, maintains on the floor or ground or tramples" the flag. The Supreme Court later overturned that law as well. In response to the government's argument that a "national consensus" had emerged across the country in favor of punishing flag burners, the Court replied: "Even assuming such a consensus exists, any suggestion that the Government's interest in suppressing speech becomes more weighty as popular opposition to that speech grows is foreign to the First Amendment."[22]

Ever since the Supreme Court's ruling in *Texas v. Johnson*, members of the U.S. House of Representatives and Senate have sought to ban flag burning through a constitutional amendment that would place such conduct outside the realm of the First Amendment. To date, no proposed amendment has received the necessary votes in Congress to be submitted to the states for ratification.

Spending as speech

Although the Supreme Court has not limited the protections of the First Amendment to political speech, speech about politics, elections, and electoral candidates is viewed by many as the core of the First Amendment. "Whatever differences may exist about interpretations of the First Amendment," the Court has stated, "there is practically universal agreement that a major purpose of that Amendment was to protect the free discussion of governmental affairs."[23]

Although most people might agree that political advocacy is protected free speech, opinion is more fractured when the question is how the government may regulate elections and electoral campaigns. For example, some say that laws limiting the amounts of money that can be spent on campaigns are in effect limits on freedom of speech. Others say that the government has a right and even a duty to ensure that elections are fair and free of undue influence, even if this means limiting conduct—such as contributing money to a candidate or spending money on campaign advertising—that furthers a political message.

The Supreme Court has made clear that limits on campaign spending are subject to First Amendment challenge. In *Buckley v. Valeo* (1976), the Court struck down parts of the Federal Election Campaign Act that limited the total amount that could be spent on federal campaigns, curbed independent spending by individuals or groups in support of candidates, and restricted how much money a candidate could contribute to his or her own campaign.

In *Buckley v. Valeo,* the Court said that in the campaign context, money is the equivalent of speech. Therefore, the government may not limit the expenditure of money, just as it may not restrict political speech:

> A restriction on the amount of money a person or group can spend on political communication during a campaign necessarily reduces the quantity of expression by restricting the number of issues discussed, the depth of their exploration, and the size of the audience reached. This is because virtually every means of communicating ideas in today's mass society requires the expenditure of money.[24]

The Court let stand limits on the amount that individuals or groups may contribute directly to a particular candidate or political committee. Limits on such contributions, the justices reasoned, were justified by the government's interest in preventing corruption and the appearance of corruption. However, the Court also said that independent expenditures by individuals or groups in support of candidates (but not directly contributed to them) were not as likely to lead to corruption as direct contributions and therefore were protected free speech. In addition, under *Buckley v. Valeo*, candidates may spend as much of their own personal funds on their own campaigns as desired.

Backers of strict campaign finance laws fear that the nation's election process is unduly influenced by money—that those who spend the most money can buy the attention and therefore the votes of the voters. Debates over proposals to amend the federal election campaign laws have become perennial features in the U.S. Congress. There is every reason to believe that neither legislators nor the courts have yet spoken the last word on this subject, but for now a candidate with a large personal fortune can spend as much of it on campaigning as he or she wishes.

Freedom of assembly

Closely related to the First Amendment's guarantee of "the freedom of speech" and its protection of expressive

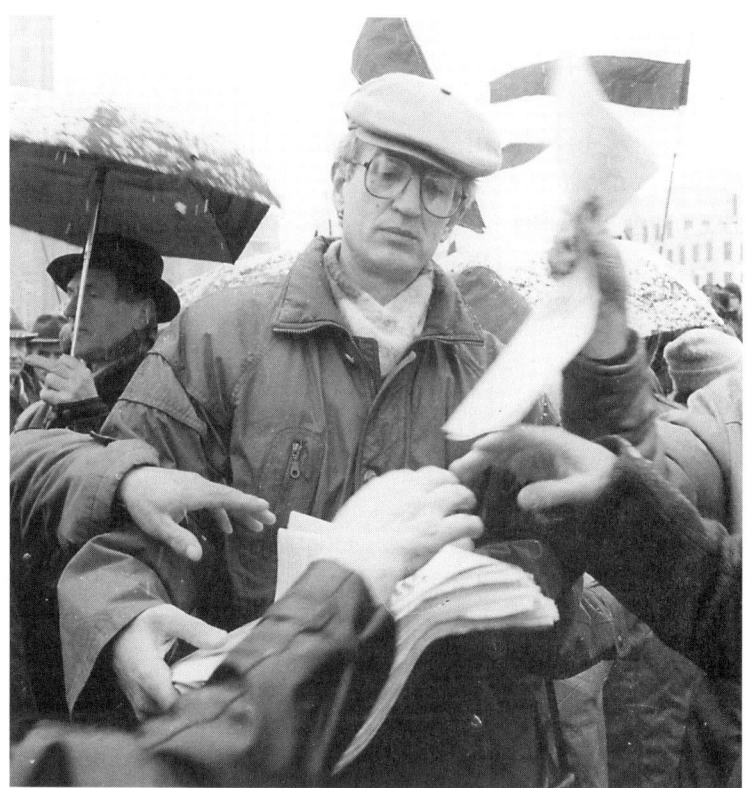

The freedom of assembly allows individuals to demonstrate, hold rallies, and distribute leaflets.

conduct is its separate promise that the government will not limit "the right of the people peaceably to assemble, and to petition the Government for a redress of grievances." Together with freedom of speech, freedom of assembly protects individuals' rights to demonstrate, hold rallies, and distribute leaflets. At times, these activities, like speech itself, may conflict with the interests of a majority of a community. A demonstration may snarl traffic, divert police from their normal tasks, and require extra work by public maintenance crews to clean up the litter left behind. Apart from these logistical issues, the majority may simply oppose demonstrations by groups whose views and causes it does not share.

In cases where local governments have tried to limit demonstrations, the Supreme Court has fashioned a rule that is intended to honor freedom of assembly while acknowledging communities' concerns about the logistical and material effects of mass gatherings. The Court has ruled that governments may place reasonable regulations on when, where, and how speakers may express themselves, but the rules must not be motivated by an effort to restrict any speaker's content. These permissible regulations are known as "time, place, and manner" restrictions, and they must be content-neutral, narrowly tailored to serve a significant government interest, and leave open alternative channels of communication. Under this approach, for example, a city may require demonstrators to obtain a parade permit or may limit demonstrations in certain places in order to protect public safety, but the restrictions must apply evenhandedly to all speakers.

Like other standards ("clear and present danger," "fighting words"), the "time, place, and manner" rule is more easily stated than applied. For example, in the spring of 1999, the city of Daytona Beach, Florida, announced a plan to restrict traffic at the annual Black College Reunion, a popular gathering of African American college students on their spring vacations. The weekend event draws tens of thousands of students. In response to complaints by Daytona Beach residents and businesses in prior years about rowdy behavior and traffic congestion, city officials said they would restrict automobile access to the city's beachfront to official permit holders—mostly residents, hotel guests, and business people. However, a federal judge ruled that the plan violated the students' right of assembly and that the city had unfairly singled out the Black College Reunion for greater restrictions than those pertaining to other events.

Restricting rallies

Similarly, in 1998, both New York City officials and the leaders of a proposed Million Youth March, at which a controversial figure named Khallid Abdul Muhammad planned to speak, had to turn to the courts to untangle their disagreements over the limits that could be placed on the rally. City officials cited traffic and security concerns in denying Muhammad's application for a permit to hold the march in Harlem but said they would not oppose alternative sites.

Explaining the city's determination to keep the Million Youth March out of Harlem, New York City mayor Rudolph Giuliani expressed concern about the possibility that Muhammad would make inflammatory remarks. In the past, Muhammad's speeches had attacked Jews, Catholics, and gays. But organizers of the march said its purpose was to encourage strength and unity among New York's black and Latino youths and to protest police brutality, job discrimination, slavery, gang violence, and the poor quality of educational opportunities.

In response to the city's refusal to issue a permit to march in Harlem, the event's organizers sued the city in federal court. U.S. District Judge Lewis Kaplan found that the city had ample means to ensure public safety at the Million Youth March and that the city's rules for issuing parade permits led to decisions that were too arbitrary to pass First Amendment muster. A federal appeals court affirmed the ruling but added that the city could place time limits on the march as well as require the demonstrators to keep within a defined six-block area.

Fighting gangs

Sometimes the reason for limiting freedom of assembly is not so much because the gathering in question is itself a menace, but rather because authorities want to discourage other conduct of those who are coming together. Legislation to prevent gang activity and public nuisances such as vagrancy, drunkenness, and aggressive begging often reflect the belief that, in an urban environment, even minor disorderly conduct contributes to violence and detracts from the quality of life. The Supreme Court, however, has exhibited sympathy for the principle that among the civil liberties protected by the First Amendment is the freedom to assemble for no reason, to wander, and even to loiter. For example, in striking down a Jacksonville, Florida, antivagrancy law in 1972, Justice William O. Douglas credited these freedoms of assembly with fostering among Americans "the feeling of independence and self-confidence, the feeling of creativity." These freedoms, he added, "have encouraged lives of high spirits rather than hushed, suffocating silence."[25]

However, the rise of gang-related urban violence in recent years has led city governments to adopt antiloitering laws to try to pry city streets from the grip of dangerous gangs. In 1992 the city of Chicago enacted a law aimed at preventing gang violence by prohibiting gatherings of gang members in public places. The law empowered police officers to disperse any group loitering "with no apparent purpose" if at least one person in the group was a suspected gang member. From 1992, until an Illinois court ruled the law unconstitutional in 1995, Chicago police arrested some forty-two thousand people under the ordinance.

Rights of gang members

According to Eileen Pahl, who represented individuals challenging the ordinance in state court, "The law penalizes people for engaging in First Amendment activities. It is not a crime to be a gang member or associate with one, just as it is not a crime to be a member of the KKK or the Shriners."[26] Pahl also indicated that while she could understand the government's desire to fight gang violence, the battle should not be carried out by laws that criminalize mere presence at a particular time and place. Added Harvey Grossman, a lawyer who challenged the law when the case went before the U.S. Supreme Court in December 1998, "When the government regulates the use of public streets, sidewalks, and parks, places historically reserved for expression, on the basis of the identity or associations of a person, the law must be narrowly tailored. It must be the least restrictive means to achieve the government's goal."[27]

In June 1999, the Supreme Court struck down the Chicago ordinance on the grounds that it was too vague to give citizens a clear idea of what they were and were not allowed to do. As the Chicago ordinance was written, opined Justice John Paul Stevens in support of the Court ruling in *Chicago v. Morales*, "It matters not whether the reason that a gang member and his father, for example, might loiter near Wrigley Field is to rob an unsuspecting fan or just to get a glimpse of Sammy Sosa leaving the ballpark; in either event, if their purpose is not apparent to a nearby police officer, she (the officer) may . . . order them to disperse."[28]

The Court's ruling was extremely fractured, including a total of six separate opinions by the justices. None of the justices said that the antigang law violated freedom of assembly, however, and only three said that liberty includes the right to wander or loiter. In biting dissent, Justice

The rights to wander and loiter are said by some to be part of society's civil liberties.

Clarence Thomas wrote, "I fear that the Court has unnecessarily sentenced law-abiding citizens to lives of terror and misery.... Today, the Court focuses extensively on the 'rights' of gang members and their companions. It can safely do so—the people who will have to live with the consequences of today's opinion do not live in our neighborhoods."[29]

The Court's divisions in *Chicago v. Morales* reflect the nation's concerns over gangs and urban violence. Many support antigang measures and want them upheld. Thirty-one states, the U.S. Conference of Mayors, and the National Governors Association filed statements supporting Chicago's ordinance with the Supreme Court. "Individual rights are important, but community needs are important, too," says Brian Stettin of the Center for the Community Interest. "Allowing gang members to exercise their full rights makes life hell for people in the area who are trying to raise a family."[30] As in other areas of constitutional conflict, the heart of the matter is where to draw the line between one individual's First Amendment freedom and another's right to be free from harm.

3
Media Freedoms

IF SPEECH BY a single individual in a single forum has the power to annoy, offend, incite, mislead, and endanger other members of society, so much more so does speech that is spread by newspapers, magazines, television, radio, books, the Internet, and record companies. At the same time, such speech also has a great capacity to exert a positive force, whether by educating and connecting people, disseminating beauty and art, or spreading ideas. The protection granted to these outlets, originally referred to as freedom of the press, today might more accurately be called media freedoms.

In recent years, the media have come under fire for producing films, music, magazines, books, and other material that many find deeply disturbing, often depicting bloody violence and graphic sex. The U.S. Congress, as well as many state legislatures, has responded to public pressures by considering, and in some cases adopting, laws to limit the availability of offensive material, whether it takes the form of music, television, movies, or sites on the World Wide Web. Such attempts to restrict media content, while supported by many Americans, are themselves under fire from people who see them as limitations on the freedom of expression guaranteed by the First Amendment.

Violent reactions

In April 1999, Eric Harris and Dylan Klebold roamed the halls of Columbine High School in Littleton, Colorado, gunning down fellow classmates and teachers before

Crosses are erected near Columbine High School commemorating the people who were gunned down by their fellow classmates.

shooting themselves to death. Their rampage left twelve other students and one teacher dead. People in the community and across the nation could not help but notice the similarities between the deadly shootings and a scene in the movie *The Basketball Diaries*, in which a character played by actor Leonardo DiCaprio methodically pumps bullets into students at a fictional high school. Similarly, in 1997, fourteen-year-old Michael Corneal opened fire on his classmates in a West Paducah, Kentucky, school, killing three students. In a subsequent lawsuit, the victims' relatives claimed that Corneal was inspired by *The Basketball Diaries* and the video game *Mortal Kombat*.

Violence in the media is a disturbing and emotional issue for many Americans. Singer Ozzy Osbourne has been sued three times by parents who claimed that the lyrics of his song "Suicide Solution" influenced their sons to kill themselves. Separately, a Louisiana convenience store clerk and her family sued the producers and director of the movie *Natural Born Killers* after two teenagers robbed the store and shot the clerk. According to the lawsuit, the teenagers went on a crime spree after repeatedly watching *Natural Born Killers* and modeled their behavior after that of a young couple depicted in the film killing dozens of people. In a similar case, the relatives of three victims murdered in 1993 by a contract killer sued the publisher of *Hit Man: A Technical Manual for Independent Contractors.* The book provides detailed advice on how to carry out a murder. The lawsuit claimed that because the murderer referred to the manual when he killed his three Maryland victims, the publisher was liable for their deaths.

Manual of violence

These lawsuits reflect the concern held by many that exposure to words and images of violence—on television, in music and movies, online, or in books and magazines—causes some people to act in destructive ways and that therefore the portrayal of violence in the media should be regulated. According to the American Psychological Association, the average American child sees eight thousand murders and one hundred thousand acts of violence on television before reaching age thirteen. Research examining whether media violence causes real-world violence is hotly debated. Studies show that some children who watch violent television shows (in a laboratory setting) react by hitting dolls or popping balloons or playing sports more aggressively. Other studies suggest that people who engage in violence tend to have a history of watching a lot of violent television, but these studies leave unanswered the critical question: Does violent television cause such people to behave aggressively, or do aggressive people simply seem to prefer violent entertainment?

Difficult as it is to determine whether media violence causes real-life violence, this determination is central to whether the government may limit such media violence under current Supreme Court rulings. The Court's decision in *Brandenberg v. Ohio* says that even speech that advocates force and violence may be limited only when it is directed at "inciting or producing imminent lawless action and is likely" to do so. Given this standard, efforts to restrict the sale or distribution of violence-laced movies and music have frequently failed. Ozzy Osbourne's suicide-promoting song lyrics have received constitutional protection. And, judges in Missouri and Tennessee have invalidated state laws aimed at limiting the sale or rental of violent videos, saying the laws were too vaguely written.

Judges have, however, declined to offer blanket protection to some media outlets. In the lawsuit brought against the publisher of *Hit Man: A Technical Manual for Independent Contractors*, a federal appeals court ruled that the First Amendment did not apply because the book is "pure and simple, a step-by-step murder manual."[31] Rather than go to trial, the publisher, Paladin Press of Boulder, Colorado, settled the case in May 1999, by agreeing to stop publishing the book. The publisher also agreed to pay millions of dollars to the families of three victims whose murderer read the book before carrying out the crimes. In the case against the movie *Natural Born Killers*, the filmmakers argued that the lawsuit "invites litigation against artists everywhere whenever criminal or demented conduct mimics artistic expression."[32] However, a Louisiana appeals court said that if, as the lawsuit alleged, the moviemakers intended to incite viewers to violence, the movie was not protected by the First Amendment. The U.S. Supreme Court let the rulings in both cases stand without comment.

Sex, speech, and the Internet

Similar to the outcry against excessive violence in the media is the revulsion of many in society to explicit descriptions and depictions of sex. One medium by which sexually explicit materials are distributed to large numbers of people is the Internet. In response to concerns that cyberspace provides children easy access to words and pictures about sex, in 1996 Congress passed the Communications Decency Act, which made it a crime to make "indecent" or "patently offensive" communications available to minors via the Internet. The Supreme Court overturned that law in 1997, finding that it placed an "unacceptably heavy burden on protected speech" that "threatens to torch a large segment of the Internet community."[33]

Congress tried again in 1998, passing the Child Online Protection Act, which focused more narrowly on commercial World Wide Websites. That law imposed criminal and civil penalties on websites that distribute material deemed "harmful to minors" without using electronically appropriate measures to deny access to young people, such as requiring a credit card number for entry. In February 1999, a federal court in Philadelphia ruled that the law was unconstitutional and blocked its enforcement. "[P]erhaps we do the minors of this country harm," U.S. District Court Judge

Lowell A. Reed Jr. wrote in his ruling, "if First Amendment protections, which they will with age inherit fully, are chipped away in the name of their protection."[34]

No one argues that the men who wrote the First Amendment actually intended to protect sexually explicit materials when they formulated the freedom of speech clause. Supreme Court cases have firmly established, however, that words and pictures about sex, including those intended to titillate rather than to inform or educate, are generally speech that is protected by the First Amendment. "[A]bove all else," the Supreme Court said in 1972, "the First Amendment means that government has no power to restrict expression because of its message, its ideas, its subject matter, or its content."[35] More specifically, in a later ruling the Court declared: "Entertainment, as well as political and ideological speech, is protected; motion pictures, programs broadcast by radio and television, and live entertainment, such as musical and dramatic works, fall within the First Amendment guarantee."[36]

Limits on sexual speech

There is one category of sexually explicit expression that is not protected by the First Amendment and upon which the government may impose limits: obscenity. According to the Supreme Court, something is obscene if it (1) appeals to the average person's prurient (shameful or morbid) interest in sex; (2) depicts sexual conduct in a "patently offensive way"[37] as defined by community standards; and (3) taken as a whole, lacks serious literary, artistic, political, or scientific value.

The Court has held also that "indecent expression" (which is defined somewhat differently than "obscenity") may be subject to some regulation, at least in the broadcasting, cable, and television media. In particular, the Court said in a 1978 ruling, the government may require radio and television stations to limit "indecent" material to hours when children are unlikely to be tuned in. Finally, the Supreme Court has allowed legislators to outlaw the sale to minors of material that is deemed harmful to them, although it might not fall into the technically defined category of "obscenity."

Given the complexity of the competing interests in controversies involving sexually explicit communications—freedom of expression, protecting children, and upholding community standards—it is not surprising that the law can produce confusing or unsatisfying results. Even the federal judge who found the Child Online Protection Act of 1998 unconstitutional expressed his "personal regret" that his ruling would "delay once again the careful protection of our children."[38] There is no denying the importance of the goal of shielding children from harmful sexual material—the challenge lies in achieving the acceptable balance between freedom and limits.

Books on trial

The desire to shield children from harmful or inappropriate influences is also at the heart of controversies in which one group—frequently parents—wishes to remove allegedly objectionable books from a school's reading list or a local library's shelves. Reasons for the objections include concerns about profanity, racist attitudes, and the promotion of beliefs or choices (such as homosexuality) with which some parents disagree. For example, Mark Twain's *The Adventures of Huckleberry Finn* has been challenged for its racist language. Two books, *Daddy's Roommate* and *Heather Has Two Mommies*, have drawn parents' ire for their sympathetic depiction of homosexuality. According to the American Library Association, the other most frequently challenged books in recent years include the *Goosebumps* series, by R. L. Stine; *I Know Why the Caged Bird Sings*, by Maya Angelou; and *It's Perfectly Normal*, by Robie Harris.

Those who object to books being pulled from library shelves or from school curricula call the practice book banning. Sometimes they use extreme comparisons and say that their opponents are engaging in totalitarian or Nazi-like tactics.

Economist Thomas Sowell offers a different perspective on the question of book banning. Libraries and schools cannot own or teach every book published, he points out. Constraints on time and money mean that they must pass over "at least 99 percent of all books." School officials, librarians, parents, and other members of a community will necessarily disagree on which books should be purchased by a school or library, yet decisions must be made. Some books are bought, some are not. This is not book "banning," he says. The books that people argue over are available in "bookstores from sea to shining sea. The government itself buys some of them. Many of these books are circulating in the tens of thousands, and some in the millions."[39]

Freedom of the press

Like other media outlets, the press—that segment of the media that reports and comments on news—is also subject to intensified criticism today. Certainly the press serves as a valuable surrogate for the public in gathering informa-

Although the First Amendment gives freedom to the press, the press is under intense criticism for abuse of that right.

tion about affairs of state and politics, and America's founders clearly intended that the freedom of the press be protected. Indeed, Thomas Jefferson considered the press so important that he once said, "Were it left to me to decide whether we should have a government without newspapers, or newspapers without a government, I should not hesitate a moment to prefer the latter."[40] But some worry that the press's intrusive methods of gathering information and its choices of sensational subject matter are harmful and out of control.

The press does have its own separate mention in the First Amendment; the text refers not only to "freedom of speech" but also specifically to "freedom of the press." The question that frequently arises is whether the press enjoys freedoms and protections under the "freedom of the press" component of the First Amendment different from the rights granted under the "freedom of speech" clause to ordinary citizens. The Supreme Court has not spoken clearly on this matter, although some of its decisions strongly indicate that the government should tread carefully when it considers regulating the press. "That the First

Amendment speaks separately of freedom of speech and freedom of the press is no constitutional accident, but an acknowledgment of the critical role played by the press in American society," Supreme Court Justice Potter Stewart wrote in a 1978 opinion. "The Constitution requires sensitivity to that role, and to the special needs of the press in performing it effectively."[41]

Government secrets

A basic function of the press is to safeguard what the Supreme Court has called the "profound national commitment to the principle that debate on public issues should be uninhibited, robust, and wide-open."[42] Central as this commitment is to the First Amendment, it can also be inconvenient and embarrassing to government officials and private individuals. Press investigations into their actions may encounter strong opposition from public officials. Perhaps the best-known example of such opposition resulted in the historic "Pentagon Papers" case, *New York Times Co. v. United States* (1971). The Pentagon Papers—the name given to the U.S. Defense Department's secret history and analysis of the country's involvement in Vietnam—were leaked to the *New York Times* and the *Washington Post*. The government claimed that publication of the papers would compromise national security and demanded that newspapers not publish them. The papers refused the government's demand and the conflict—with claims of freedom of the press competing with claims of national security interests—went to the Supreme Court.

In *New York Times Co. v. United States*, the Supreme Court ruled that any governmental attempt to prevent the press from publication "comes to this Court bearing a heavy presumption against its constitutional validity," and as Justice Potter Stewart said in his concurring opinion in that case, a "prior restraint" of the press may be justified only if publication would "surely" result in "direct, immediate, and irreparable"[43] harm to the nation.

In a 1931 ruling, the Supreme Court created a limited exception to the idea that prior restraint is harmful: "No one would question but that a government might prevent actual obstruction to its recruiting service or the publication of the sailing dates of transports or the number and location of troops."[44] This ruling has become known as the "national security exception" to the general rule against prior restraints. In the Pentagon Papers case, the first time the Supreme Court was called upon to apply the exception in the forty years since its 1931 formulation, a majority of the justices found that publication did not threaten national security, and the newspapers were free to publish.

Because of the general distaste for prior restraints, courts are not frequently called upon to address them. Federal, state, and local authorities, knowing that they are unlikely to win a censorship case against the press, rarely attempt to apply such restraints.

Courtroom coverage

Ironically, although courts frequently rule in favor of the press when the executive branch of government is involved, the courts themselves—including judges, prosecutors, plaintiffs, and defendants—may also try to erect obstacles to press coverage of certain proceedings. Courtrooms in the United States (except for juvenile courts, where young offenders are protected from publicity) have traditionally been open to the public, and the Supreme Court has ruled that the First Amendment guarantees the press a right of access to criminal proceedings and criminal case files.

Despite the general practice of open courtrooms, judges may bar reporters from pretrial proceedings in certain criminal cases or "seal" documents (that is, make them unavailable to the public) where secrecy is needed to protect a criminal defendant's right to a fair trial. The concern is to minimize the type of pretrial publicity that might prejudice the public and potential jurors against the defendant or might give the prosecution information to which it is not entitled. For example, in the pretrial proceedings of the defendants who were charged in the highly publicized 1995 bombing of the Alfred P. Murrah Federal Building in

Oklahoma City, U.S. District Court Judge Richard Matsch ordered papers sealed to prevent disclosure of evidence to the press or public.

Although a defendant's right to a fair trial is the most widely recognized reason for closing criminal proceedings and documents to the press, some judges have denied access to the press to protect jurors as well. For example, in the 1997 trial of a young woman accused of attempting to extort $40 million from comedian Bill Cosby, a federal judge sealed the transcript of a closed hearing to protect a juror's privacy "in light of the intense media attention"[45] focused on the case. In some cases, judges have also issued orders forbidding reporters from seeking to interview jurors after a criminal trial is over, in the name of juror privacy. The Supreme Court has not ruled on these practices.

Libelous liberties

Perhaps the most notable area in which the Supreme Court has given the press special treatment due to its historically important role in American society is libel law. Libel, or defamation, is a legal claim in which one individual alleges that another's words have damaged his reputation. In general, courts have long held that a person may sue another for libel (and claim money damages) if the sued party has

Evidence in the highly publicized trial of the Oklahoma City bombing was sealed to prevent disclosure to the press and public.

published words or pictures that are false and defamatory. A publication is considered defamatory if it tends to hold a person up to ridicule, contempt, shame, or disgrace.

However, in *New York Times Co. v. Sullivan* (1964), the Supreme Court altered the law of libel dramatically, specifically for the purpose of protecting the press. The First Amendment, the justices found, required a change in the traditional law of libel to give the press room to make errors without fear of liability when reporting on public officials. In that case, supporters of Martin Luther King Jr. had placed a full-page advertisement in the *New York Times* complaining about the treatment of civil rights demonstrators by city officials in Montgomery, Alabama. Some of the statements in the ad were false, and Montgomery's police commissioner, L. B. Sullivan, sued the newspaper for libel in Alabama state court and won a large amount of money from an all-white local jury.

In reversing the libel award against the *New York Times*, the Supreme Court held that the First Amendment shields the press from libel suits brought by public officials, even for statements that are false and defamatory. In its opinion, written by Justice William Brennan, the Court ruled:

> The constitutional guarantees require, we think, a federal rule that prohibits a public official from recovering damages for a defamatory falsehood relating to his official conduct unless he proves that the statement was made with "actual malice" —that is, with knowledge that it was false or with reckless disregard of whether it was false or not.[46]

Justice William J. Brennan also wrote for the Court, "erroneous statement is inevitable in free debate," and "it must be protected if the freedoms of expression are to have the 'breathing space' that they 'need . . . to survive.'"[47]

In later cases, the Supreme Court extended this shield to statements about "public figures" who do not hold office (but whose activities exposed them to the media's spotlight) and to issues of "public interest" involving private citizens. For example, under the "public figure" theory, supermarket tabloids such as the *National Enquirer* and the *Globe* enjoy some protection from lawsuits by the celebrities they tend to cover, even when they print erroneous statements or rumors about them.

Digging for data—or dirt?

Because the Supreme Court has protected the press in its leading rulings on libel law, some judges and legislators have devised new legal theories to provide individuals a means to prevent or be compensated for harm to reputation and invasion of privacy by news media. For example, an individual may sue the press under the claim of "disclosure of private facts" for having published personal information that is (1) intimate, (2) highly offensive, and (3) of no legitimate public concern.

Although the Supreme Court has made clear that the press should be restrained from publication only in the most extreme circumstances, in recent years, lower courts have issued a surprising number of prior restraints based on state privacy law. Aggressive news-gathering techniques have become particularly vulnerable. For example, in 1996, reporters for the television program *Inside Edition* took videotapes of the chief executive of a large health maintenance organization (HMO) and his family. One of the tactics used by the *Inside Edition* camera crew was to anchor a boat in a public waterway outside the family's Florida estate and to use the boat as a platform from which to film the house, using a telephoto lens and a highly sensitive microphone.

Inside Edition justified the reporters' actions by explaining that the videotape was for a story about the excessive salaries and rich lifestyles of some HMO executives. When the family sued the journalists, a federal district judge ordered the television crew to stop its activities. The judge acknowledged the importance of a news story on the HMO industry but denied that the *Inside Edition* crew was engaging in the type of activity protected by the First Amendment. The information and pictures were sought, he said, not "for the legitimate purpose of gathering and broadcasting the news, but to try to obtain entertaining background for their TV expose."[48]

Restraining reporters

Should the activities of the press be granted less protection when they seem to be more akin to producing entertainment than gathering news? One problem with this approach, argues Richard S. Hoffman, a Washington, D.C., lawyer who represents media clients, is that "When courts try to distinguish between news and entertainment, they ignore established precedent. In a 1948 ruling, the Supreme Court said that the line between 'informing' and 'entertaining' is too hard to define to serve as the boundary between protected and non-protected First Amendment press activity."[49] Judge Richard Posner of the U.S. Court of Appeals for the Seventh Circuit has also observed,

> Today's "tabloid" style investigative television reportage, conducted by networks desperate for viewers in an increasingly competitive television market . . . constitutes—although it is often shrill, one-sided, and offensive and sometimes defamatory—an important part of that market. It is entitled to all the safeguards with which the Supreme Court has surrounded liability for defamation.[50]

Not everyone agrees with these conclusions. Some judges, outraged by what they view as unacceptably intrusive press tactics, have issued orders to stop such invasions and to allow the targets of the media focus to sue for damages. An appeals court in California recently said a woman who was injured in a car accident could sue the show *On Scene: Emergency Response* because the show's cameraman videotaped her after emergency medical technicians placed her inside a rescue helicopter. In 1995 another state appellate court in Sacramento said that a television station and its news crew could be liable for inflicting severe emotional distress by telling three children they found on a playground that two of their playmates had been murdered.

A free press is one of the hallmarks of American society. Many would say that a free press is essential to a free country. But individual autonomy and privacy are also closely held American values, values that are frequently threatened by a free press. When these interests collide, courts, lawmakers, and society must make difficult choices.

4

Religious Liberties

THE CLASHES BETWEEN competing rights that characterize the Bill of Rights in operation come into particularly sharp focus in the field of religious liberties. This is because the Bill of Rights expressly protects two very different forms of religious liberty which often are at odds with each other.

"Congress shall make no law respecting an establishment of religion," the First Amendment says, "or prohibiting the free exercise thereof." The purpose of the first clause, known as the Establishment Clause, is to prevent the government from setting up an official or government-favored religion. This clause has also come to stand for the separation of church and state—for the proposition that the government must not become too entangled in religion, even short of setting up an official religion. The second clause, the Free Exercise Clause, prohibits the government from interfering with individuals' right to worship as they choose (or not to worship at all).

The Establishment Clause and the Free Exercise Clause can clash with one another when, for example, individuals seek government support, funding, or facilitation for their religious practices. Is such government action an impermissible "establishment" of religion—or is it a permissible step toward ensuring that individuals are able to exercise their religion freely? A similar question is raised when individuals seek to be excused from the requirements of an otherwise applicable law, claiming that it hampers their right to exercise their faith freely. An important consideration in all such cases is whether, and at what point, the government's accommodation of religious beliefs or practices rises to the level of an impermissible "establishment" of religion.

The right to be different

The Free Exercise Clause forbids the government from outlawing religious belief or from making an individual's exercise of religion unreasonably difficult. In the second half of the twentieth century, the U.S. Supreme Court handed down a series of decisions establishing the boundaries that the government must respect when it takes actions that affect religious practices. For example, in a case in which the Court said the state could not force an Amish parent to send his children to school after eighth grade, Chief Justice Warren Burger wrote: "A way of life that is odd or even erratic but interferes with no rights or interest of others is not to be condemned because it is different."[51]

Difficulties arise, however, because some religious practices that seem "odd" may also have a socially negative impact on others, particularly children. One of the

Amish children cannot be forced to go to school after the eighth grade due to religious practices.

thorniest questions in this area concerns religions that reject medical care, relying instead on "faith-healing" for the treatment of illnesses. According to a recent report by the American Academy of Pediatrics and a national nonprofit group called Children's Healthcare Is a Legal Duty (CHILD), 172 children in the United States have died in the past twenty years after their parents refused to obtain medical treatment for them due to religious objections. The report concluded that in 140 of these cases the children would have had at least a 90 percent chance of recovery had they received medical care.

Ordinarily, a parent who does not seek medical care for a seriously ill child can be charged with child abuse or neglect. However, according to CHILD, forty-one states have special laws that exempt parents from child abuse or neglect charges if the harm was a result of a religiously based refusal to obtain medical treatment. As a spokesman for the Christian Science Church in Oregon explained recently in a newspaper column, members of his faith seek "within law, reasonable accommodation allowing for responsible spiritual healing."[52] However, when three children in Oregon whose parents were members of the Followers of Christ Church (which is not affiliated with the Christian Science Church) died in 1998 after their parents did not get medical assistance for them, the American Academy of Pediatrics and CHILD called for a nationwide repeal of faith-healing exemption laws.

Those seeking to hold parents accountable when the failure to obtain medical care for their children results in physical harm argue that the Free Exercise Clause of the First Amendment should not be used to the detriment of children. The right to believe freely, they say, should not include the right to act in a medically unacceptable manner. "The Christian Science and other faith-healing groups have a right to practice their religion to a point," Rita Swan, president of CHILD declared in an interview, but "religious belief shouldn't give you the right to deprive a child of needed medical care." A Christian Science spokesman countered: "Christian Science has a 130-year record of healing children through spiritual practices. It would be incorrect to say you can't practice your religion anymore, and spiritual healing is the cornerstone of our religion."[53]

When parents have been prosecuted for their failure to get medical attention for their children, the outcomes have varied. In a 1997 case in Pennsylvania, the parents of sixteen-year-old Shannon Nixon were found guilty of involuntary manslaughter after Shannon died of untreated diabetes because her Faith Tabernacle congregation believed that God, not medicine, cures illness. But in a similar case, involving Christian Scientists who did not seek medical care for their two-year-old who subsequently died of a bowel obstruction, the Massachusetts Supreme Judicial Court said that the state's religious exemption statute (which has since been repealed) relieved the couple of legal responsibility. The U.S. Supreme Court has not yet ruled directly in a faith-healing case.

The peyote case

Although the freedom to *believe* whatever one wishes is absolute and unlimited, the freedom to *practice* one's belief may be subject to some governmental regulation despite the Free Exercise Clause. Of course, today the government rarely targets specific religious conduct in legislation. However, laws that govern other conduct may incidentally affect and restrict religious practice. In these situations, the Supreme Court has ruled that some regulation of religious practice may be permitted.

The question of where a lawful government regulation ends and an unlawful breach of the Free Exercise Clause begins has been the subject of particularly intense debate and activity since 1990. In that year, the Supreme Court upheld Oregon's denial of unemployment benefits to two members of the Native American Church who had been fired from their jobs for smoking peyote. Peyote is a hallucinogen which has been used in Native American religious practices for centuries. Justice Antonin Scalia, writing the Court's opinion in *Employment Division v. Smith*, noted that previous rulings "never held that an individual's religious beliefs excuse him from compliance" with a government action or law that might incidentally infringe on a person's religious beliefs or practices. What the Free Exercise Clause protects against, Justice Scalia wrote, are government actions and laws created with the intent to regulate religious actions or beliefs. "It would doubtless be unconstitutional, for example," Justice Scalia said, "to ban the casting of 'statues that are to be used for worship purposes,' or to prohibit bowing down before a golden calf."[54] Since peyote was prohibited for everyone, the opinion concluded, the government was not singling out a particular religion for discriminatory treatment.

The decision in *Employment Division v. Smith* created an upheaval among religious groups, civil liberties advocates, and constitutional law scholars, some of whom said it struck a serious blow against religious liberty. For years, many had assumed that the First Amendment prohibited the government from both intentional and unintentional discrimination when its regulations affect religious practices. The problem with the *Smith* test, according to critics, is that the government rarely intends to discriminate against religion, but unintentional discrimination does just as much harm to religious freedom. Some argue that, under the Supreme Court ruling, the government could adopt regulations applicable to the public at large that have the effect of outlawing the use of wine in religious ceremonies or interfering with the implementation of Jewish laws regarding kosher meats. By enforcing rules of general applicability without regard to religious practices, these critics argue, public school officials could deny students permission to take time off for religious holidays or forbid them from wearing religious clothing such as yarmulkes.

Legislating religious rights

Persuaded by a broadly based coalition of interest groups—including such unlikely allies as the liberal People for the American Way and the conservative Christian Coalition, as well as religious denominations of all stripes—Congress passed the Religious Freedom Restoration Act of 1993. That law prohibited the government—federal, state, or local—from restricting a person's religious practices unless it had a "compelling interest" in the restriction and used the "least restrictive means" possible in regulating religious practice. Mark E. Chopko, general counsel for the U.S. Catholic Conference, said the law gave religious people "the right to insist that accommodation, not conformity, be the norm."[55]

But soon the civil liberties pendulum swung again. Under the new law, opponents argued, people could use religion as an excuse for ignoring laws intended to promote and protect society. Indeed, according to the *New Republic* magazine, the Religious Freedom Restoration Act (RFRA) was invoked by prison inmates in 189 lawsuits claiming the right, based on religious grounds, to be free from prison regulations. The claims ranged from suits by prisoners who had been denied permission to wear crucifixes to one prisoner's claim to a right to smoke marijuana because of his membership in the Church of Marijuana.

The freedom to practice one's belief may sometimes be subject to government regulation.

But it was a property dispute, not a prisoner's claim, that brought RFRA to the Supreme Court. In 1995, the Catholic archbishop of San Antonio applied for a permit to enlarge a church in the town of Boerne, Texas. The local zoning board turned down the request because the enlargement would violate the city's historic preservation law. The archbishop sued, arguing that RFRA required the city to exempt the church from its historic preservation laws.

In June 1997, the Supreme Court overturned the Religious Freedom Restoration Act. Its decision, *Boerne v. Flores*, invalidated RFRA because Congress had radically changed the meaning of religious liberty and impermissibly assumed the role of a court when it effectively rewrote the Court's ruling in the earlier peyote case. As had occurred when the Court handed down its 1990 decision in *Employment Division v. Smith*, the 1997 *Boerne v. Flores* ruling generated considerable controversy. "The decision is an obvious setback for religious liberty," said Walter Weber, counsel at the American Center for Law and Justice, a Christian organization. Weber told the online publication *Free!*, "I think it highlights the need for a federal religious-liberty amendment. The Smith decision severely limited religious freedom in this country, and six justices today said the Congress can't fix that. Therefore, I believe the Constitution needs to be fixed."[56]

Others who are also disappointed with the *Boerne v. Flores* ruling, however, believe that states have the power to "fix" the religious liberty problem. They advocate the passage of state laws to protect religious freedom. By 1998, nearly half the states had proposed, and in some instances passed, RFRA-like legislation. Whether these laws will withstand challenges in court remains to be seen.

The church-state "wall"

The Free Exercise Clause guarantees a right to exercise one's religion freely. But the Establishment Clause tempers that freedom by denying religion a right to preferential treatment by the government, even when special treatment would enhance the free exercise of religion. In a

1947 case, the Supreme Court said, "In the words of Jefferson, the clause against establishment of religion by law was intended to erect 'a wall of separation between church and state.' "[57] The separation of church and state does not reflect the Constitution's hostility to religion, but rather the belief that religion is best protected when it is outside the scope of governmental interference, even interference of a supportive nature.

Courts have invoked the Establishment Clause to strike down state support for parochial schools, statutes mandating school prayer, and the exhibition of religious displays such as nativity scenes and menorahs on public property. As such rulings make plain, the Establishment Clause is violated when the government takes action with respect to religion even if the action falls short of actually "establishing" an official religion. To help the public and courts determine when the wall between church and state has been impermissibly breached, the Supreme Court formulated a three-part test in a 1971 case, *Lemon v. Kurtzman*. The *Lemon* test, which still applies today, asks whether the governmental action or policy at issue (1) has a religious purpose, (2) serves primarily to advance or endorse religion, or (3) fosters excessive government "entanglement" with religion. A "yes" answer to any one of the three questions means that the government action or policy violates the Establishment Clause.

Religion in school

One of the most visible arenas in which the interpretation of the Establishment Clause has been at issue is the nation's public school system. Controversies have arisen and continue to rage over both prayer (or prayerlike interludes) and religious instruction in public schools. Another contentious issue concerns public funding for religious schools, including school voucher programs that give public funds to parents to send their children to religious schools. These conflicts bring to the forefront the split between the two religion clauses of the First Amendment.

In 1962 the Supreme Court ruled against officially sponsored and organized school prayer. The following year, the

Court held that Bible readings in public schools also violate the First Amendment. In a later case, going still further, the Court struck down a requirement that students begin the school day with a moment of silence (during which the students were expected to pray). More recently, in 1992, the Court found that even a nondenominational prayer offered at public school graduation ceremonies ran afoul of the Establishment Clause.

In the school graduation case, *Lee v. Weisman*, the Court explained why it found even nonsectarian school prayers inconsistent with the First Amendment. Prayers in school as well as at a school-sponsored ceremony such as graduation are inherently coercive, the Court indicated, even when students are not required to participate. "The prayer exercises in this case are especially improper," the Court's opinion declared, "because the State has in every practical sense compelled attendance and participation in an explicit religious exercise at an event of singular importance to every student, one the objecting student had no real alternative to avoid."[58] The Court also noted that school sponsorship of prayers at a graduation ceremony entangles government and religion—exactly what the Establishment Clause forbids. The meaning of the First Amendment, the Court said, is that "religious beliefs and religious expression are too precious to be either proscribed or prescribed by the State."[59]

On the other hand, the Free Exercise Clause guarantees that religious people, including students, may pray privately and read religious materials. The Court's rulings mean that these religious activities may not be sponsored by the public school system. Students may pray or read holy scriptures on their own time during the school day. They may also pray before meals and tests and discuss religion with other students.

Many people disagree with the Court's rulings on school prayer. Voluntary prayer in school does not violate the Establishment Clause, they argue, because it does not force nonbelievers to participate. Moreover, they say, nondenominational prayer in the classroom and at school events encourages a child's moral development. Others argue that a prohibition of school prayer interferes with students' rights to worship freely as guaranteed by the First Amendment's Free Exercise Clause.

Efforts to introduce prayer in schools and at school events continue, despite the Court's decisions. In recent years, for example, many schools across the country have seen the rise of student-initiated prayer, in which students, rather than teachers or other school officials, promote and lead prayers in the classroom and at school events. At least one federal court of appeals, the U.S. Court of Appeals for the Fifth Circuit (whose rulings apply in Texas, Louisiana, and Mississippi) has upheld the constitutionality of "student-initiated" high school graduation prayer where a majority of the graduating class have requested that a student volunteer offer a prayer at the school's commencement ceremony.

Teaching religion

The content of what public schools teach—particularly their curricula relating to the origins of humanity—has been, and continues to be, another subject of intense contention under the Establishment Clause. One of the most famous trials in U.S. history was the so-called "Monkey Trial" in 1925, which pitted famed lawyer Clarence Darrow against the charismatic Democratic politician William Jennings Bryan. Tennessee, like a handful of other states and numerous school boards at the time, prohibited the teaching of Charles Darwin's theory of evolution in the public schools. John T. Scopes, a twenty-four-year-old biology teacher in a rural Tennessee town, challenged the law. Scopes's lawyer was Clarence Darrow; William Jennings Bryan represented the state in prosecuting Scopes. Scopes was convicted of violating the Tennessee law, but the Tennessee Supreme Court later reversed the conviction on a technicality.

Forty years after *Tennessee v. Scopes*, another teacher challenged a law similar to the one under which John Scopes had been prosecuted. In 1965, Susan Epperson, a

H	O	S	G	M

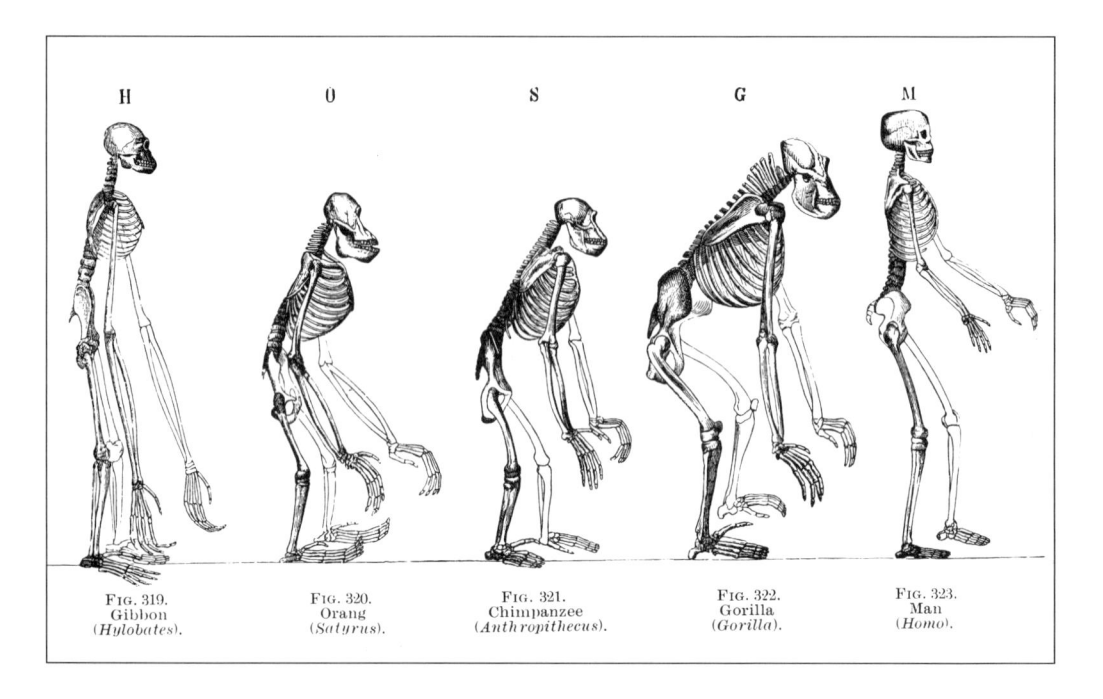

FIG. 319.
Gibbon
(*Hylobates*).

FIG. 320.
Orang
(*Satyrus*).

FIG. 321.
Chimpanzee
(*Anthropithecus*).

FIG. 322.
Gorilla
(*Gorilla*).

FIG. 323.
Man
(*Homo*).

Teaching the theory of evolution in schools has been the topic of much debate and trial.

twenty-four-year-old high school teacher in Little Rock, Arkansas, challenged the state's 1928 statute that imposed criminal penalties for teaching that modern humans evolved from earlier animals. Epperson wanted to use a high school biology textbook which said humans and apes may have had a common ancestor in the remote past. The trial court in Epperson's case found the state law unconstitutional; on appeal, the U.S. Supreme Court agreed, finding that the ban on teaching the theory of evolution violated the Establishment Clause.

If states or local public schools could not prohibit the teaching of evolution, the question still remained whether they could at least require that the competing, religious view of the origins of humankind—sometimes called *creationism* or *scientific creationism*—be included in the curriculum. Advocates for this approach argue that religious people have a right under the Free Exercise Clause of the First Amendment to "equal time" for the discussion of scientific creationism in the classroom. At the urging of these advocates, two states, Arkansas and Louisiana, adopted laws requiring the teaching of "creation science" in public school classrooms where evolution is taught. The Arkansas law was struck down by a federal judge in 1982. A challenge to the Louisiana law went all the way to the Supreme Court. In 1987, the Court held that the law violated the Establishment Clause because "the preeminent purpose of the Louisiana legislature was clearly to advance the religious viewpoint that a supernatural being created humankind."[60] Justice Antonin Scalia and Chief Justice William Rehnquist dissented, arguing that the law merely required the teaching of an alternative scientific theory and that there was "ample uncontradicted testimony that 'creation science' is a body of scientific knowledge rather than revealed belief."[61]

Public money for private schools

According to the U.S. Census Bureau, approximately one of out every ten students in the United States attends private, rather than public, school. Because they are not owned or operated by the government, private schools are free to allow, and even require, their students to engage in religious studies and prayer. Unlike public schools, which are paid for by the government (using taxpayer dollars) and do not charge tuition, private schools are not government-funded and generally must charge tuition. Some parents who might like to send their children to private schools do not do so because they cannot afford the tuition.

To increase the opportunities for more students to attend private schools—and in response to people who believe that the nation's public schools are failing either to impart moral values to their students or to lay a solid academic foundation—some states have adopted school voucher programs under which parents may obtain government money to send their children to private schools. These programs are thought by opponents to violate the Establishment Clause because they constitute government aid to religion. Defenders of these programs say they merely broaden educational opportunities for children, and they also point out that not all government aid to religious schools violates the Establishment Clause. Pennsylvania, for example, spends tens of millions of dollars on textbooks and services, such as speech therapy and testing, for students in private schools. New Jersey spends a like amount on books, nursing, and other services for private school students, including those with disabilities. Supporters of such state government spending say it is justified by a 1968 Supreme Court ruling, which said that a state could pay for textbooks for nonreligious studies for students in parochial schools.

The U.S. Supreme Court has not yet decided directly whether school voucher programs are permissible under the Establishment Clause. In June 1998, however, the Supreme Court of Wisconsin upheld the Milwaukee Parental Choice Program, which provides low-income children the opportunity to use state education funds in private schools, including religious schools. Wisconsin Justice Donald Steinmetz wrote for the court that the program did not violate the Establishment Clause because "it has a secular purpose, it will not have the primary effect of advancing religion, and it will not lead to excessive entanglement between the state and participating sectarian private schools."[62] Voucher advocates hailed the decision as a commonsense application of the First Amendment. Voucher opponents, citing the ruling as a danger to the separation of church and state, appealed the decision to the U.S. Supreme Court, which declined to review the case.

Private beliefs, public life

Besides limiting the ability of public school officials to implement religious beliefs in the classroom, the Establishment Clause also applies outside the school setting when government officials seek to implement or display symbols of religious beliefs in government buildings and on government property. For example, in 1989 the Supreme Court ruled that a city could not set up a Christmas crèche in the local courthouse carrying a banner proclaiming "Glory to God in the Highest." In a different case, however, the Court upheld Pawtucket, Rhode Island's nativity scene, which was displayed along with nonreligious Christmas symbols, including a Christmas tree and Santa Claus house. The difference between the two cases was that in the former the display put up by the city sent what the Court called a "patently Christian message,"[63] which violated the Establishment Clause. The government may display holiday symbols that are primarily nonreligious, such as Santa Claus and Christmas trees, but it may not put up a display that "has the effect of endorsing or disapproving religious beliefs."[64]

Implements of religious beliefs may be displayed as long as they do not endorse or disapprove of others' beliefs.

Calls for change

Given the controversy surrounding the Supreme Court's interpretation of the Constitution's religion clauses, it is not surprising that some lawmakers have tried to overturn those rulings through legislation. Efforts to overrule the Supreme Court through ordinary legislation can be problematic, because under the U.S. Constitution, the Supreme Court has the role of interpreting the meaning of provisions of that document and the Bill of Rights. Because of this limitation on what Congress can achieve through legislation, some members of Congress have proposed amending the Constitution itself.

Although the exact text of various proposed constitutional amendments has varied, generally they seek to permit prayer in school and to allow more governmental funding of activities carried out by religious organizations. To date, the measures have not garnered the votes in Congress necessary to send them on to the states for ratification.

More than two centuries ago, commenting on the then-proposed Constitution, James Madison observed that religious belief was one of the major issues that "divided mankind into parties, inflamed them with mutual animosity, and rendered them much more disposed to vex and oppress each than to co-operate for their common good."[65] Today, more than 90 percent of Americans profess a belief in God. Surveys indicate that more than half of all Americans say they pray at least once a day, and more than 40 percent report that they have attended worship services during the previous week. Also, the United States is far more religiously diverse now than it was in 1787, with more than fifteen hundred different religious bodies and sects, and 360,000 churches, mosques, and synagogues. These factors—widespread faith plus cultural diversity—combine to ensure continuing controversies over religious freedoms and make the First Amendment's religion clauses as important today as they were when America was founded.

5

The Right to Privacy

BENEATH THE SURFACE of nearly all discussions of civil liberties, there lies a silent partner—the notion that individuals are entitled to a measure of autonomy and noninterference from both the government and from the world around them. Freedom of expression, freedom of the press, freedom of religion: These are all about the right to say to the government, "Let me be."

This right to be left alone, however, is not only a component of the written liberties guaranteed by the Bill of Rights. It has also become accepted as a constitutional guarantee in its own right—the "right to privacy." Over the years, the U.S. Supreme Court has ruled that the right to privacy includes both the right to make certain fundamental decisions (relating in particular to family matters) without governmental interference and to avoid forced disclosure to the government of personal matters.

Although neither the Constitution nor the Bill of Rights mentions anywhere a right to privacy, since the 1890s courts have said that this right is implied. For example, the Fourth Amendment's "right of the people to be secure in their persons, houses, papers, and effects" and its protection against "unreasonable searches and seizures" has sometimes been described as an example of an individual's unwritten right to keep certain parts of his or her private life free from governmental interference. And, starting in the 1920s, the Supreme Court found that the "liberty" protected by the Constitution's Fifth and Fourteenth Amendments—which say that no person may be deprived of "life, liberty, or property" without "due process of law"—includes parents' rights to keep the government out of at least some decisions regarding their children's education.

In a 1965 ruling striking down a Connecticut law that prohibited the use of contraceptives and the dispensing of information about birth control to married couples, Justice William O. Douglas said the Constitution created "zones of privacy" that protect against "governmental invasions of the sanctity of a man's home."[66] The Connecticut law at issue in that case, he said, violated a "marital right of privacy." Two years later the Court struck down a state law forbidding interracial marriages, ruling that "liberty" includes the freedom to marry whom one chooses. In 1972 Justice William Brennan said, "If the right to privacy means anything, it is the right of the *individual*, married or single, to be free from unwarranted governmental intrusion into matters so fundamentally affecting a person as the decision whether to bear or beget a child."[67]

The assertion of a constitutional right to privacy has led to some of the most heated controversies concerning civil liberties. This is not because people disagree on whether privacy is a good thing. The difficulty is that, as a right that is not specified in the Constitution or Bill of Rights, "privacy" is particularly susceptible to competing claims about its validity and meaning. "I like my privacy as well as the next one," Justice Hugo Black wrote in dissent in the 1965 Connecticut contraceptive case, "but I am nevertheless compelled to admit that the government has a right to invade it unless prohibited by some specific constitutional provision."[68]

However, Justice Black's view has not prevailed. A few years later, the question was no longer whether a right to privacy existed—the Supreme Court said it did—but what the right encompassed. In particular, the question was whether the right to privacy included a woman's right to obtain an abortion without governmental interference. This has been, and continues to be, the most socially and politically divisive issue—not only in privacy law, but in all of constitutional law—during the last quarter of the twentieth century.

The right to an abortion

The historic case in which the Supreme Court ruled that the right to privacy guarantees a woman's right to an abortion is *Roe v. Wade* (1973). The author of the opinion in that case, Justice Harry Blackmun, said that the Court's earlier rulings "made clear that only personal rights that can be deemed 'fundamental' or 'implicit in the concept of ordered liberty,' are included in this guarantee of personal privacy." In the past, Justice Blackmun observed, the Court had found that activities relating to marriage, contraception, family relationships, child rearing, and education were "fundamental" or "implicit in the concept of ordered liberty," and therefore protected by the right to privacy. Then he concluded that abortion, too, deserved constitutional protection: "This right of privacy ... is broad enough to encompass a woman's decision whether or not to terminate her pregnancy."[69]

As is the case with other civil liberties, the right to an abortion is not absolute. In *Roe v. Wade* the Court acknowledged that the state also has important interests when a woman chooses to have an abortion: "[A] state may properly assert important interests in safeguarding health, in maintaining medical standards, and in protecting potential life. At some point in pregnancy, these respective interests become sufficiently compelling to sustain regulation of the factors that govern the abortion decision."[70] To guide the public and the states in determining when regulation was permissible, Justice Blackmun announced a trimester scheme. Under this framework, the government had no right to interfere with a woman's right to choose an abortion during the first three months of a pregnancy. During the fourth through sixth months (the second trimester), the government's interest was sufficient to support regulations aimed at protecting the health of the mother. The right to an abortion was weakest, and the government's right to regulate greatest, in the final trimester, when the fetus is presumably "viable," or able to live outside the womb.

The *Roe v. Wade* decision could be seen as an inevitable sequel to the Court's earlier opinions finding a "zone of

The landmark case of Roe v. Wade has sparked controversy not only about the right to an abortion, but also the right to privacy.

privacy" surrounding an individual's actions and thoughts concerning procreation and family. But this is not a unanimous view. Many agree with Justice (later Chief Justice) William H. Rehnquist's dissent in *Roe v. Wade* that the right to an abortion is not "so rooted in the traditions and conscience of our people as to be ranked as fundamental."[71] And, if the right to an abortion is not fundamental, this argument goes, it does not belong within the scope of the right to privacy.

Evolving standards

Roe v. Wade was not the last word on a woman's right to an abortion. In the years that followed, the Supreme Court struck down state laws requiring that a woman obtain her husband's consent to an abortion and that she wait twenty-four hours between her consultation about her pregnancy with a health care provider and the abortion itself. The Court ruled, however, that other regulations did not violate a woman's right to an abortion, including a law that denied federal funding for abortions and a rule that required two doctors to be present during abortions performed in the third trimester. Laws regulating abortions obtained by minors have produced several Supreme Court rulings that appear somewhat inconsistent. One decision struck down a requirement that both parents of a minor must consent to her abortion. Another decision upheld a different parental consent law that allowed judges to excuse the consent requirement.

By the late 1980s, the Court's attitude toward the abortion right had become extremely uncertain. The composition of the Supreme Court had changed, with most of the justices who decided *Roe v. Wade* retired or deceased. *Roe v. Wade*'s trimester approach to regulating abortion was under attack, on medical as well as legal grounds. In a 1992 case, *Planned Parenthood v. Casey*, the Court did away with the *Roe v. Wade* trimester framework, finding that the ban on regulating abortions in the first three months of pregnancy did not give enough weight to the state's legitimate interest in potential life. But the Court, while badly divided, upheld the central finding of *Roe v. Wade* that the concept of individual liberty, and the right to privacy, included the right to an abortion. "It is a promise of the Constitution that there is a realm of personal liberty which the government may not enter," Justice Sandra Day O'Connor wrote for the Court. "At the heart of liberty is the right to define one's own concept of existence, of meaning, of the universe, and of the mystery of human life."[72]

In *Planned Parenthood v. Casey*, the Supreme Court announced a new standard for evaluating abortion regulations, one that upheld a right to an abortion while providing the state more leeway than before in protecting its interests. Under *Planned Parenthood v. Casey*, a law regulating abortion is unconstitutional only if it puts an "undue burden" on the woman seeking the procedure. The states may implement regulations that make abortion more difficult to obtain or more expensive; they may not, however, pass laws that create a truly substantial obstacle to obtaining an abortion.

Today, the right to an abortion remains part of the right to privacy. However, the controversy is by no means over. The noisy social and political debate continues, in legislatures, in the streets, and in voting booths. More quietly, but just as importantly, the legal debate continues. Supporters of a broad right to privacy hold on to its affirmation in *Planned Parenthood v. Casey*—while opponents wait for the day when perhaps their narrower view of the right to privacy, and broader view of the rights of a fetus, might prevail.

Medical matters

Just as individuals might wish to draw a curtain of privacy around their decisions regarding procreation and abortion—the beginnings of life—so might they wish to shield their decisions about the end of life. Choices about when and how to discontinue medical treatment and life support are obviously extremely personal. One's choices are likely

Under Planned Parenthood v. Casey, *states are allowed to implement regulations that make an abortion difficult to obtain, but they may not cause an "undue burden."*

to reflect one's ideas about the meaning of life and what constitutes a meaningful life. Other personal issues such as religious faith and family relationships are also central to end-of-life decisions. On the other hand, society and the government have an interest in ensuring that health care providers (in whose hands end-of-life decisions are often placed) maintain the highest possible standards of medical care and ethics. Society may rightly take steps to protect its most vulnerable members and ensure, for example, that patients are not denied treatment or care simply because it is cheaper to let them die. As with abortion, the question is where to strike a balance between society's interest in human life and the individual's right to make highly personal decisions about medical care and, ultimately, death.

The "right to die"

Ironically,—and adding to the difficulty of the issue—this question often arises in situations where an individual whose "right to die" is being asserted can no longer speak for himself or herself. The leading case in this area involved Nancy Cruzan, who was twenty-five years old in early 1983 when she lost control of her car on a country road outside a small Missouri town and crashed. The accident left her permanently unconscious, in a condition known as a "persistent vegetative state." Nancy lost any ability to think, feel, make voluntary movements, or communicate. She had no awareness of the world around her. All that remained of her brain's ability to function was its control over breathing, heartbeat, and circulation.

Because she was unconscious, Nancy was unable to eat or swallow, so three weeks after the tragedy, in February 1983, doctors inserted a tube into her stomach to enable her to receive nutrition and medication. Without this artificial feeding tube, Nancy would have died.

In 1987, after four and one-half years of watching their daughter languish in a state of permanent unconsciousness, with no realistic hope of improvement, Nancy's parents asked a Missouri judge for permission to remove her feeding tube. The Cruzans emphasized their daughter's total unawareness of herself and her surroundings. They said that prior to the accident she had told friends that she would not want to be kept alive unless she could live normally.

The Cruzans' request was granted by a state court judge. But before the tube was removed, the Missouri Supreme Court reversed that decision and denied the family's request. From there, the legal wrangling over Nancy Cruzan's death seemed to take on a life of its own. While Nancy lay in a state of silent suspended animation, the people around her—parents, friends, doctors, caretakers, lawmakers, clergymen, judges, writers—were anything but silent. The debate over her condition and fate swept the nation.

Mercy or murder

Ten thousand people are estimated to be in persistent vegetative states in this country. Like Nancy, nearly all of them lapsed into unconsciousness without having left instructions or even any meaningful indication of the type of life-support care they would desire. Some say that people in a permanently unconscious state, such as Nancy Cruzan, are disabled and that to remove such a person's feeding tube is no different than starving a disabled person to death. In addition, they argue, allowing the euthanasia, or "mercy killing," of a permanently unconscious person is a dangerous precedent, which could easily lead to killing of people who are somehow "undesirable."

Those who advocate the "right to die"—and who say that an unconscious person's right to choose death may be exercised by his or her loved ones or by trusted physicians—insist that people who are permanently unconscious cannot be compared to those with disabilities. According to one Minneapolis neurologist who examined Nancy Cruzan, "It's kind of a cruel hoax that nature and medical technology have played on us"—the body still functions, but the person "is not really there at all."[73]

The right-to-die issue pertains as well to people who *are* conscious and *can* knowingly express a preference to end their lives. A person born today can expect to live, on average, seventy-seven years, compared to forty-six years for a person born in 1900. As people live longer, inevitably, more will suffer from lingering terminal illnesses that cause enormous discomfort. More still will suffer from nonterminal, but chronic, conditions that cause them equal misery. And, many will suffer from conditions that are non-life-threatening but that sap them of their will to live. How should society respond to requests from such people who want the assistance of another—sometimes a family member, sometimes a doctor—to commit suicide?

In 1990, the U.S. Supreme Court issued a decision in the case of *Cruzan v. Director of Missouri Department of Health* that gave something to both sides of the issue. The Court ruled that an individual *does* have a right to refuse life-sustaining treatment, including food and water. But when the case involves a person, such as Nancy Cruzan, who has become unconscious without expressing preference on the question, a state may (as Missouri did) require "clear and convincing evidence" of that person's desire to discontinue life support before allowing doctors or family to terminate such treatment.

A few months after the Supreme Court's ruling, Nancy Cruzan's parents went back to state court armed with more evidence that their daughter would have preferred death to living in a persistent vegetative state. The judge heard from three friends of Nancy's, as well as her doctor, who had previously opposed removing the feeding tube. This time Nancy Cruzan's parents received the permission they sought. On December 15, 1990, the tube through which Nancy received nutrition and water was removed. She died twelve days later, on December 27. Nancy's family said in a written statement: "Knowing Nancy as only a family can, there remains no question that we made the choice she would want."[74] Protesters, who had gathered outside Nancy's hospital, had a different perspective. As Nancy Cruzan lay dying inside, they held a vigil, singing Christmas carols and demonstrating with hand-lettered signs. One sign read simply: "Mercy or Murder?"[75]

Although the questions raised by the Nancy Cruzan case are by no means completely settled, many advocates

When individuals record their instructions about providing or withholding medical care, questions of their right to die may be easier to answer.

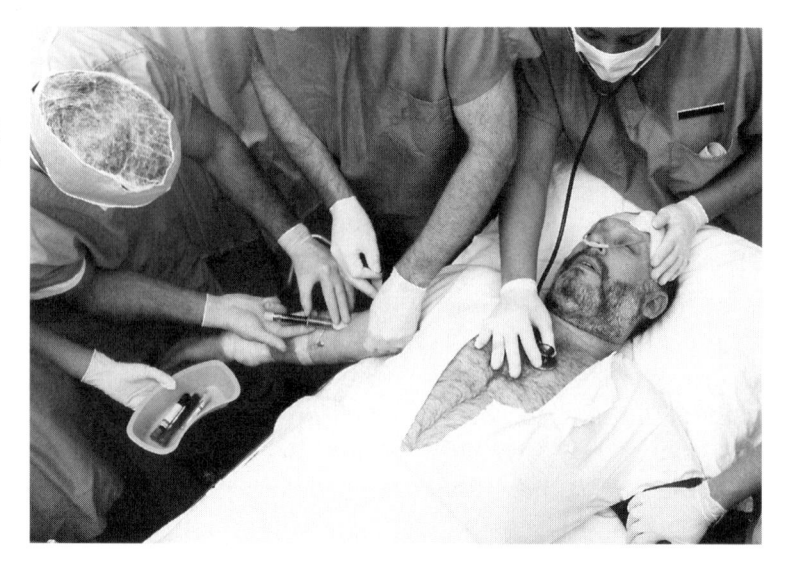

on both sides of the right-to-die question have focused their attention on the practical aspects of the issue rather than on courtroom resolutions. Organizations such as the New York–based Society for the Right to Die urge individuals to formally record their instructions about the providing or withholding of care in various medical situations. Many doctors believe that better care, pain management, and better counseling of patients and their families can help avert the types of legal crises that result in cases such as Nancy Cruzan's.

Assisted suicide

Two 1997 Supreme Court rulings on physician-assisted suicide may also prompt participants in the right-to-die debate to seek solutions outside the courtroom. Federal appeals courts in New York and Washington had ruled that there is a constitutional right to die with the aid of a doctor and struck down laws banning physician-assisted suicide in those states. The Supreme Court disagreed and upheld the laws. Those attacking the right-to-die bans argued that the high Court's rulings in *Cruzan* and in abortion cases supported the right of a mentally competent, terminally ill adult to hasten death with the aid of a physician (in the form of a prescription for a lethal dose of medicine).

In the 1997 cases, the Court clarified its earlier rulings. *Cruzan*, the justices said, stood for the principle that a competent person has a constitutionally protected interest in refusing unwanted medical treatment, but that is not the same as a constitutional right to die. As for the analogy to a woman's right to abortion, the Court said that not every important, intimate, and personal decision is protected by the Constitution—only those that are deeply rooted in the nation's history. A constitutional right to assisted suicide, Chief Justice William H. Rehnquist wrote, far from being a deeply rooted liberty, would reverse centuries of legal doctrine and practice. Anglo-American common law has punished or otherwise disapproved of assisting suicide for hundreds of years.

Despite Chief Justice Rehnquist's reading of the history of assisted suicide, several other justices, concurring separately in the physician-assisted suicide cases, held open the possibility that a person might have a right to assisted suicide in certain circumstances. Justice Sandra Day O'-Connor said the Court had not foreclosed the possibility that "a mentally competent person who is experiencing great suffering has a constitutionally cognizable [understood] interest in controlling the circumstances of his or her imminent death."[76] For now, however, by declining to find that the freedom to commit physician-assisted suicide is protected by the Constitution, the Court left the decision to ban or permit such suicide up to the states. Only Oregon has adopted a law (enacted by voter referendum) that allows physician-assisted suicide in certain limited and carefully regulated circumstances.

Prying eyes—and more

Debates over the right to die and abortion concern the manner in which a constitutional right to privacy shields personal decisions from governmental interference. When people think of privacy, however, they probably have in mind a more literal concept: keeping prying eyes and ears out of their private lives.

An important source of protection from governmental intrusions on individual privacy is the Fourth Amendment to the U.S. Constitution, which says that "the right of the people to be secure in their persons, houses, papers, and effects, against unreasonable searches and seizures, shall not be violated." The scope of the Fourth Amendment's privacy protection arises, for example, when police search a person's home or subject an individual to a body search. The Fourth Amendment is also at issue when police conduct traffic checkpoints at which they stop and search motorists. The Supreme Court has even ruled that government-ordered testing of workers' blood and urine for drug use is a "search" covered by the Fourth Amendment.

The question underlying all Fourth Amendment privacy disputes is whether a particular action amounts to a "search." The Supreme Court has indicated that, generally, a search is conducted when the government invades an individual's reasonable expectation of privacy. Sometimes the question of what constitutes a "search" can lead to surprising results. For example, a person's front or back yard is "searched" if police poke around in it—but only if the yard is not too large. The Supreme Court has ruled that individuals enjoy a zone of privacy immediately outside their homes, in the "area [that] harbors the intimate activity associated with the sanctity of a man's home and the privacy of life."[77] But the Court found that no search had occurred when police walked along a footpath on a man's Kentucky farm and discovered marijuana growing in open fields that were not visible from the public road. The fact that the farmer posted "No Trespassing" signs all around his property line and protected his land with a locked gate did not transform the police action into a "search," according to the Court.

Similarly, the Supreme Court has found that police surveillance of a person's backyard from a helicopter flying four hundred feet above ground to observe a marijuana crop was not a "search"; the overflight did not invade a reasonable expectation of privacy. And, because people put trash out at curbside for strangers to take away to the dump or recycling center, the Court has determined that garbage is not protected by a reasonable expectation of privacy—so when the police go through a person's trash cans looking for incriminating evidence, they are not engaged in a search.

To satisfy the Fourth Amendment, a search itself must be reasonable. Generally, courts determine reasonableness by balancing the government's need to search against the invasion of privacy involved. Some searches seem flagrantly unreasonable—such as the strip searches (including body-cavity searches) carried out by the Chicago police as a matter of policy on every woman arrested, even for a traffic violation, until the practice was declared unconstitutional by two federal courts in the early 1980s.

Other cases are closer calls. For example, in 1990 the Supreme Court upheld the constitutionality of using traffic checkpoints to stop and search drivers at random. Some civil liberties advocates argued that checkpoints are opportunities for the police to harass innocent motorists. But the

Court said that any invasion of privacy and inconvenience was justified by the evidence that checkpoints reduce alcohol-related fatalities on the road.

With respect to government-ordered drug testing of employees—an important civil liberties issue among those who work in the public sector—the Supreme Court addressed the reasonableness of such programs in the late 1980s. Concerned about safety on the nation's rail system, the Federal Railroad Administration wanted railroads to require their employees to take blood, breath, and urine tests for drugs and alcohol. All these tests were "searches"; the question was whether the government's concerns about safety justified testing in the absence of any suspicion that the employees were under the influence of alcohol or drugs. In *Skinner v. Railway Labor Executives' Association*, the Court said such tests were constitutional because of the seriousness of the threat to public safety presented by alcohol- or drug-impaired railway workers. In a companion case, the Court also upheld suspicionless drug tests of government employees who were applying for positions directly involving the interdiction of illegal drugs or the carrying of firearms. Where public safety arguments have been less convincing, however, courts have struck down programs that randomly tested police officers, firefighters, teachers, civilian army employees, prison guards, and other employees of government agencies.

To be lawful under the Fourth Amendment, a police search must be reasonable under the circumstances.

Keeping secrets

Sometimes, of course, what people want kept private is information about themselves. The Supreme Court has recognized that the Constitution also protects another type of privacy, which it called "the individual interest in avoiding disclosure of personal matters."[78] In a 1977 case, the Court confirmed an individual's constitutional right to prevent the government from disclosing personal matters about him or her. This case involved a New York law which required the recording of the name, address, and age of every patient obtaining certain prescription drugs. Patients argued that disclosing their names violated their privacy and deterred them from seeking needed medical treatment. While the Court agreed that individuals have a constitutional interest in avoiding disclosure of personal matters, the justices upheld the New York law because the state used safeguards to maintain the secrecy of these records. At the same time, however, the Court indicated that the issue is still open to debate: "We are not unaware of the threat to privacy implicit in the accumulation of vast amounts of personal information in computerized data bases or other massive government files."[79]

The Supreme Court has not revisited the issue, but a number of lower federal courts have held that individuals have a constitutional right to privacy regarding medical information. Still, disclosure of personal health information is a growing concern across the nation. A person's medical records may be protected by the traditional doctor-patient privilege or by statute—New York and California law, for example, bar disclosure of HIV test results without a patient's consent. But in many ways such records are an open book. Colorado, for example, requires doctors to report to the government all persons who test positive for HIV so that government employees may notify an infected person's sex partners of their risks.

Another way in which medical privacy may be breached is through the health insurance industry. To obtain medical insurance, an individual generally must authorize release of his or her medical records to the insurance company in question. Insurance companies frequently pool information through the Boston-based Medical Information Bureau (MIB), which contains data on some 15 million Americans and Canadians.

Serious though they may be, these breaches of privacy (as well as disclosures made possible through other computer databases and, of course, the Internet) generally do not involve an individual's constitutional civil liberties. The battleground for preventing widespread disclosure of private information is, for the most part, nonconstitutional territory because the disclosures are not made or required by the government. As a result, federal, state, and local legislators face increasing pressures to strengthen laws and regulations to protect individual privacy from nongovernmental invasion.

Concerns have also been growing about privacy in the workplace, as more and more employers conduct surveillance of their employees, including reading e-mail and monitoring employees at their desks, and as more employers require their employees to participate in drug testing. Few laws limit the ability of private employers, as opposed to the government, to require employees to submit to blood and urine tests. While such tests may appear to invade workers' privacy, some employers feel they are justified. Companies that pay for their workers' health insurance may feel they are entitled to information that will help them control the insurance costs for high-risk individuals (such as smokers and drug users). Employers also worry about being held liable in lawsuits for the wrongful actions of their employees. To protect themselves, they seek information to weed out workers whose backgrounds suggest they are likely to engage in harmful or illegal acts.

Protecting individual civil liberties

It seems unlikely that lawmakers and courts can ever completely catch up to the capabilities of technology and human ingenuity to pry personal information out of its remaining hiding places. To some degree, the loss of control over personal information may be an unavoidable cost of living in the information age. A 1995 study conducted by a privacy expert at the University of Illinois found that two-thirds of the large corporations polled disclose personal information about their employees to creditors who request such information. Nearly half said they gave employee information to landlords. The study's author, Professor David Linowes, observed: "With information being transmitted across the country and abroad at the speed of light, an error in one record can be propagated a hundredfold instantaneously."[80]

But America's history of debate over civil liberties suggests that the apparent loss of control over privacy is neither irreversible nor irremediable. After all, the price of living in a representative democracy could have been that the majority's wishes always prevailed over the minority's. The Bill of Rights, however, altered that equation in favor of protecting individual civil liberties. Similarly, the price of creating a government that is not tied to an official religion could have resulted in a system that is hostile to religion. Instead, the religion clauses of the First Amendment guarantee a government that is tolerant of all religions.

This pattern of potential threats, offset by the balancing of interests under the Bill of Rights, repeats itself in every arena in the realm of civil liberties. If privacy resembles other civil liberties that Americans hold dear, lawmakers, judges, and ordinary citizens can be expected to work toward striking a balance between an information-hungry society and a population of privacy-starved individuals who want only to be left alone.

Notes

Introduction

1. Quoted in T. Harry Williams, ed., *Abraham Lincoln: Selected Speeches, Messages, and Letters.* New York: Rinehart and Winston, 1957, p. 264.

Chapter 1: The Scope of Civil Liberties

2. *Olmstead v. United States*, 277 U.S. 438, at 478 (1928) (dissenting opinion).

3. Brooke A. Masters and David Nakamura, "Library's Internet Filtering Is Barred," *Washington Post*, November 24, 1998, pp. A1, A16.

4. American Civil Liberties Union Briefing Paper Number 1, *Guardian of Liberty: American Civil Liberties Union*, 1997. www.aclu.org.

5. The Communitarian Network, *The Responsive Communitarian Platform: Rights and Responsibilities.* www.gwu.edu/~ccps/RCPlatform.html.

6. "How Casper, Wyo., reconciled rights of protesters, funeral-goers," Associated Press, October 23, 1998. www.freedomforum.org.

7. Memorandum for the U.S. Secretary of Education and the U.S. Attorney General from William J. Clinton, July 12, 1995, quoted in *First Amendment Cyber-Tribune*. www.trip.com/FACT/1st.pres.rel.html.

8. Quoted in "Mississippi Mother Wins School Prayer Challenge Before U.S. Judge," American Civil Liberties Union Press Release, June 3, 1996. www.aclu.org.

Chapter 2: Freedom of Speech and Assembly

9. *Abrams v. United States*, 250 U.S. 616, at 630 (1919).

10. Ellen Alderman and Caroline Kennedy, *In Our Defense:*

The Bill of Rights in Action. New York: William Morrow, 1991, p. 32.

11. *Abrams v. United States*, at 630.

12. Quoted in American Civil Liberties Union Briefing Paper Number 10, *Freedom of Expression*, 1997. www.aclu.org.

13. *Schenck v. United States*, 249 U.S. 47, at 52 (1919).

14. *Chaplinsky v. New Hampshire*, 315 U.S. 568, at 572 (1942).

15. *Brandenberg v. Ohio*, 395 U.S. 444, at 447 (1969).

16. Quoted in Rene Sanchez, "Abortion Foes' Internet Site on Trial," *Washington Post*, January 15, 1999, p. A3.

17. "Antiabortion Web Site Sued," *Washington Post*, January 8, 1999, p. A8.

18. Paul McMasters, "Nuremberg Files anti-abortion site: Free speech or hit list?" *Free!*, January 19, 1999. www.freedomforum.org.

19. *Tinker v. Des Moines Independent Community School District*, 303 U.S. 503 (1969).

20. *Texas v. Johnson*, 491 U.S. 397, at 399 (1989).

21. *Texas v. Johnson*, at 414.

22. *U.S. v. Eichman* and *U.S. v. Haggerty*, 496 U.S. 310, at 318 (1990).

23. Quoted in Bruno Leone, ed., *Free Speech*. San Diego: Greenhaven Press, 1994, p. 151.

24. *Buckley v. Valeo*, 424 U.S. 1, at 19 (1976).

25. *Papachristou v. City of Jacksonville*, 405 U.S. 156, at 164 (1972).

26. Quoted in Tony Mauro, "Chicago's anti-gang law to face Supreme Court scrutiny," *Free!*, April 21, 1998. www.freedomforum.org.

27. Statement of Harvey Grossman, Legal Director, ACLU of Illinois, ACLU Supreme Court Preview: 1998 Term, *City of Chicago v. Jesus Morales, et al*, ACLU Press Release, October 1, 1998. www.aclu.org.

28. *Chicago v. Morales*, U.S. Supreme Court, No. 97-1121 (June 10, 1999).

29. *Chicago v. Morales.*

30. Quoted in Mauro, "Chicago's anti-gang law to face Supreme Court scrutiny."

Chapter 3: Media Freedoms

31. David Hudson, "Appeals court lets decision stand in *Hit Man* case," *Free!*, December 17, 1997.

32. "Supreme Court won't free filmmaker from lawsuit over pair's crime spree," Associated Press, March 8, 1999. www.freedomforum.org.

33. *Reno v. ACLU*, U.S. Supreme Court, No. 96-511 (1997).

34. Quoted in John Schwartz, "U.S. Judge Blocks Law Curbing Online Smut," *Washington Post*, February 2, 1999, p. A2.

35. *Police Department v. Mosley*, 408 U.S. 92, at 95 (1972).

36. *Schad v. Borough of Mount Ephraim*, 452 U.S. 61, at 65 (1981).

37. *Miller v. California*, 413 U.S. 15, at 24 (1973).

38. Quoted in Schwartz, "U.S. Judge Blocks Law Curbing Online Smut," p. A2.

39. Thomas Sowell, "Books Are Not Being Banned," in Byron L. Stay, ed., *Censorship*. San Diego: Greenhaven Press, 1997, p. 71.

40. Quoted in Alan M. Dershowitz, *Taking Liberties*. Chicago: Contemporary Books, 1988, p. 61.

41. *Houchins v. KQED*, 438 U.S. 1, at 17 (1978) (concurring opinion).

42. *New York Times Co. v. Sullivan*, 376 U.S. 254, at 270 (1964).

43. *New York Times Co. v. United States*, 403 U.S. 713, at 714, 730 (1971).

44. *Near v. Minnesota*, 283 U.S. 697, at 716 (1931).

45. Quoted in Reporters Committee for Freedom of the Press, *The Privacy Paradox: Court Access*. www.rcfp.org.

46. *New York Times Co. v. Sullivan*, at 279–80.

47. *New York Times Co. v. Sullivan*, at 271.

48. *Wolfson v. Lewis*, 924 F. Supp. 1413, at 1432 (E.D. Pa. 1996).

49. Interview with Richard S. Hoffman, quoting *Winters v. New York*, 333 U.S. 507 (1948).

50. *Desnick v. American Broadcasting Cos.*, 44 F. 3d 1345, 1355 (7th Cir. 1995).

Chapter 4: Religious Liberties

51. *Wisconsin v. Yoder*, 406 U.S. 205, at 224 (1972).

52. Quoted in Jeremy Leaming, "Oregon lawmakers to reconsider regulations that protect faith-healing parents," *Free!*, January 27, 1999. www.freedomforum.org.

53. Quoted in Jeremy Leaming, "Groups call on states to dump exemptions for faith-healing parents," *Free!*, June 12, 1998. www.freedomforum.org.

54. *Employment Division v. Smith*, 494 U.S. 872, at 877–79 (1990).

55. Quoted in Jeremy Leaming, "Restoration drama: Downfall of federal religious-protection law produces new coalition strategy," *Free!*, April 9, 1998. www.freedomforum.org.

56. Quoted in Leaming, "Restoration drama."

57. *Everson v. Board of Education*, 330 U.S. 1, at 15–16 (1947).

58. *Lee v. Weisman*, 505 U.S. 577, at 589 (1992).

59. *Lee v. Weisman*, at 598.

60. *Edwards v. Aguillard*, 482 U.S. 578, at 591 (1987).

61. *Edwards v. Aguillard*, at 634.

62. Quoted in Jeremy Leaming, "Vouchers remain contentious issue in debate over government aid to religion," First Amendment Center, October 21, 1998. www.freedomforum.org.

63. *County of Allegheny v. ACLU*, 492 U.S. 573, at 601 (1989).

64. *County of Allegheny v. ACLU*, at 592–93.

65. Clinton Rossiter, ed., *The Federalist Papers*. New York: The New American Library of World Literature, 1961, p. 79 (Federalist No. 10).

Chapter 5: The Right to Privacy

66. *Griswold v. Connecticut*, 381 U.S. 479, at 485–86 (1965).

67. *Eisenstadt v. Baird*, 405 U.S. 438, at 453 (1972).

68. *Griswold v. Connecticut*, at 510.

69. *Roe v. Wade*, 410 U.S. 113, at 152–53 (1973).

70. *Roe v. Wade*, at 162–65.

71. *Roe v. Wade*, at 174.

72. *Planned Parenthood v. Casey*, 112 S. Ct. 2791, at 2805, 2807 (1992).

73. Quoted in Don Colburn, "Another Chapter in the Case of Nancy Cruzan," *Washington Post*, October 16, 1990, Health Section.

74. Quoted in Malcolm Gladwell, "Woman in Right-to-Die Case Succumbs," *Washington Post*, December 27, 1990, p. A3.

75. See photo accompanying Gladwell, "Woman in Right-to-Die Case Succumbs."

76. Quoted in Joan Biskupic, "Unanimous Decision Points to Tradition of Valuing Life," *Washington Post*, June 27, 1997, p. A1.

77. *United States v. Dunn*, 480 U.S. 294, at 300 (1987).

78. *Whalen v. Roe*, 429 U.S. 589, at 598 (1977).

79. *Whalen v. Roe*, at 605.

80. "Many Companies Fail to Protect Confidential Employee Data," Electronic Privacy Information Center Press Release, April 22, 1996. www.epic.org/privacy/workplace/linowesPR.html.

Organizations to Contact

The following organizations are concerned with civil liberties. The issues they address include freedom of expression, freedom of the press, religious liberties, and the right to privacy.

American Civil Liberties Union (ACLU)
125 Broad St., 18th Floor
New York, NY 10004-2400
(212) 549-2500
www.aclu.org

The ACLU is a 275,000-member public interest group devoted to protecting civil liberties. It has affiliates in every state, as well as staff attorneys who collaborate with volunteer lawyers in handling nearly six thousand cases annually. The ACLU has national projects focused on specific issues including arts censorship, privacy and technology, reproductive freedom, and children's rights.

American Library Association (ALA)
50 E. Huron St.
Chicago, IL 60611
(800) 545-2433
www.ala.org

The American Library Association works to educate the public about the importance of intellectual freedom and free speech in libraries. The ALA tracks books that are challenged in schools and libraries because some find them offensive.

Electronic Frontier Foundation (EFF)
1550 Bryant St., Suite 725
San Francisco, CA 94103-4832
(415) 436-9333
www.eff.org

The Electronic Frontier Foundation works to protect civil liberties, including privacy and freedom of expression, in the field of computers and the Internet. As an advocate for the rights of users of online technologies, EFF gets involved in litigation in which online civil liberties are at issue, conducts research and educational programs, and works to urge Congress to adopt policies that favor broad public access to information.

Electronic Privacy Information Center (EPIC)
666 Pennsylvania Ave. SE, Suite 301
Washington, D.C. 20003
(202) 544-9240
www.epic.org

The goal of the Electronic Privacy Information Center is to focus public attention on emerging civil liberties issues, including those arising out of the development of cyberspace. EPIC works to defend privacy and the First Amendment, publishes a newsletter on civil liberties in the information age, and engages in litigation to protect civil liberties in cyberspace.

The Freedom Forum
1101 Wilson Blvd.
Arlington, VA 22209
(703) 528-0800
www.freedomforum.org

The Freedom Forum is dedicated to free press, free speech, and other First Amendment freedoms. It pursues its interests through conferences, educational activities, publishing, broadcasting, online services, and other programs. Among other programs, the Freedom Forum operates the Newseum, an interactive museum about journalism and the press, in

Arlington, Virginia, and the First Amendment Center at Vanderbilt University in Nashville, Tennessee.

Institute for Justice (IJ)
1717 Pennsylvania Ave. NW, Suite 200
Washington, D.C. 20006
(202) 955-1300
www.ij.org

The Institute for Justice offers itself as an alternative to the American Civil Liberties Union for those seeking to protect individual liberty and to promote free market solutions and limited government. Calling itself the nation's only "libertarian public interest law firm," the IJ pursues litigation in defense of civil liberties such as freedom of religion and freedom of speech.

National Campaign for Freedom of Expression (NCFE)
918 F St. NW, # 609
Washington, D.C. 20004
(202) 393-2787
www.ncfe.net

The National Campaign for Freedom of Expression is dedicated exclusively to defending First Amendment rights as applied to the arts in the United States. The organization is a network of artists, arts organizations, and concerned citizens seeking to protect and extend freedom of artistic expression and fight censorship. NCFE pursues its goals through educational programs and advocacy.

National Coalition Against Censorship (NCAC)
275 Seventh Ave.
New York, NY 10001
(212) 807-6222
www.ncac.org

The National Coalition Against Censorship is an alliance of more than forty organizations, including literary, artistic, religious, educational, professional, labor, and civil liberties groups. NCAC works to educate its member organizations and the public at large about the dangers of censorship and promotes freedom of thought and expression. Among the groups that make up NCAC's membership are the American Federation of Teachers, the International Reading Association, the National Education Association, the Student Press Law Center, and the American Jewish Congress.

People for the American Way
2000 M St. NW, Suite 400
Washington, D.C. 20036
(202) 467-4999
www.pfaw.org

People for the American Way works to protect the principles of the U.S. Constitution through educational programs, public advocacy, and litigation. The focus of the organization's efforts in the civil liberties arena is on such issues as freedom of expression and religious liberty. People for the American Way monitors censorship in the nation's schools and reports its findings in a publication entitled *Attacks on the Freedom to Learn*.

Reporters Committee for Freedom of the Press
1101 Wilson Blvd., Suite 1910
Arlington, VA 22209
(800) 336-4243
www.rcfp.org

The Reporters Committee for Freedom of the Press began in 1970 as a small group of journalists in Washington, D.C., concerned with one *New York Times* reporter's struggle to fight against governmental interference in his newsgathering efforts. Today it is a major national and international resource on free speech and free press issues. The committee has played a role in the significant press freedom cases that have come before the U.S. Supreme Court, as well as in hundreds of cases in other federal and state courts.

Rutherford Institute
1445 East Rio Rd.

Charlottesville, VA 22901
(800) 225-1791
www.rutherford.org

Established in 1982, the Rutherford Institute is a not-for-profit organization with a network of more than one thousand volunteer lawyers across the United States. The institute is dedicated to defending civil liberties and human rights. Its lawyers represent individuals who have suffered discrimination because of their beliefs.

The Thomas Jefferson Center for the Protection of Free Expression
400 Peter Jefferson Pl.
Charlottesville, VA 22911-8691
(804) 295-4784
www.tjcenter.org

The Thomas Jefferson Center is a not-for-profit organization devoted to the defense of free expression in all its forms, from music to the mass media to individual artists. Each year the Center awards "Jefferson Muzzles" to individuals or organizations deemed responsible for egregious affronts to free expression. It also bestows the William J. Brennan Award to those who show extraordinary devotion to the principles of free expression.

Suggestions for Further Reading

Ellen Alderman and Caroline Kennedy, *In Our Defense: The Bill of Rights in Action*. New York: William Morrow, 1991. Two lawyers examine the Bill of Rights by telling the stories of controversies that have arisen under each of the first ten amendments to the Constitution.

Ellen Alderman and Caroline Kennedy, *The Right To Privacy*. New York: Alfred A. Knopf, 1995. Through case studies, the authors examine privacy as it is protected and threatened by law enforcement, the press, in the workplace, and in other arenas.

Charles P. Cozic, ed., *Civil Liberties*. San Diego: Greenhaven Press, 1994. A wide spectrum of views are presented on the right to privacy, limits on free expression, separation of church and state, and protection of civil liberties.

Alan M. Dershowitz, *Taking Liberties*. Chicago: Contemporary Books, 1988. The well-known Harvard law professor subtitles this collection of previously printed newspaper columns *A Decade of Hard Cases, Bad Laws, and Bum Raps*. His book examines civil liberties and defendants' rights through the perspective of cases and controversies in the news.

J. Edward Evans, *Freedom of Religion*. Minneapolis, MN: Lerner, 1990. This survey of the history of religious freedom includes accounts of important Supreme Court cases that have interpreted the religion clauses of the First Amendment.

Nat Hentoff, *Free Speech for Me—but Not for Thee: How the American Left and Right Relentlessly Censor Each Other*. New York: HarperCollins, 1992. The author, a popular columnist on the Constitution and civil liberties, reports on contemporary free speech conflicts, including book censorship and speech codes.

Peter Irons, *The Courage of Their Convictions: Sixteen Americans Who Fought Their Way to the Supreme Court*. New York: Free Press, 1988. Political-science professor and lawyer Peter Irons writes about the ordinary Americans who went to extraordinary lengths to protect their civil rights and liberties in sixteen cases that went all the way to the Supreme Court.

Peter Irons and Stephanie Guitton, eds., *May It Please the Court*. New York: New Press, 1993. This collection of transcripts of twenty-three live recordings of landmark cases as argued before the U.S. Supreme Court includes such important civil liberties precedents as *Abington School District v. Schempp, Edwards v. Aguillard, Wisconsin v. Yoder, Roe v. Wade, Bowers v. Hardwick*, and more.

Bruno Leone, ed., *Free Speech*. San Diego: Greenhaven Press, 1994. This collection of articles debating issues relating to free speech includes discussions of government funding for the arts, speech codes on college campuses, and pornography.

Victoria Sherrow, *Freedom of Worship*. Brookfield, CT: Millbrook Press, 1997. This brief book discusses the history of the Bill of Rights' guarantee of religious freedom and why this right is important today.

Byron L. Stay, ed., *Censorship*. San Diego: Greenhaven Press, 1997. All sides of various issues relating to censorship—limiting sexually harassing speech, government funding of arts, school and library censorship, antipornography laws, and more—are examined in this collection of essays and articles.

Works Consulted

Books

James MacGregor Burns and Stewart Burns, *A People's Charter: The Pursuit of Rights in America.* New York: Alfred A. Knopf, 1991. This work by two historians examines the origins and making of the Bill of Rights, Supreme Court rulings, and laws that constitute the American commitment to citizens' civil liberties.

J. M. Coetzee, *Giving Offense: Essays on Censorship.* Chicago: University of Chicago Press, 1996. This collection of essays addresses censorship in contexts ranging from political dissent to pornography.

John Dewey, *Freedom and Culture.* Buffalo, NY: Prometheus Books, 1989. A volume in the "Great Books in Philosophy" series, this book presents Dewey's views on how freedom of inquiry, tolerance of diverse opinions, cultural pluralism, and free speech all contribute to social development.

Owen M. Fiss, *The Irony of Free Speech.* Cambridge, MA: Harvard University Press, 1996. This Yale Law School professor argues that certain types of speech—hate speech, pornography, campaign expenditures—can overwhelm and silence other speech, and therefore government restrictions on such silencing speech can be defended in terms of the First Amendment.

Phillip W. Hammond, *With Liberty for All: Freedom of Religion in the United States.* Louisville, KY: Westminster John Knox Press, 1998. The author argues that the Constitution protects the convictions of individual Americans regardless of whether or not those convictions are explicitly religious.

Robert Emmet Long, ed., *Rights to Privacy*. New York: H. W. Wilson Company, 1997. This volume in a series known as "The Reference Shelf" contains reprints of articles and excerpts from books on the right to privacy, including issues concerning privacy in the information age, privacy in the workplace, and privacy and medical records.

Jonathan Rauch, *Kindly Inquisitors: The New Attacks on Free Thought*. Chicago: University of Chicago Press, 1993. The author favors unfettered speech, even hurtful speech, arguing that efforts to protect people's feelings leads to control of knowledge by central authorities.

Clinton Rossiter, ed., *The Federalist Papers*. New York: The New American Library of World Literature, 1961. Alexander Hamilton, John Jay, and James Madison published these eighty-five essays anonymously under the pen name Publius, between 1787 and 1788.

T. Harry Williams, ed., *Abraham Lincoln: Selected Speeches, Messages, and Letters*. New York: Rinehart and Winston, 1957. Abraham Lincoln's writings are arranged by date, with explanatory notes.

Articles

Associated Press, "Federal appeals court denies further review of student-led prayer decision," January 28, 1999. www.freedomforum.org.

Associated Press, "Federal judge blocks Florida city's plan to restrict Black College Reunion traffic," April 9, 1999. www.freedomforum.org.

Associated Press, "Federal judge throws out federal law limiting campaign spending," February 22, 1999. www.freedomforum.org.

Associated Press, "Government defends Christmas' status as federal holiday," October 13, 1998. www.freedomforum.org.

Associated Press, "How Casper, Wyo., reconciled rights of protesters, funeral-goers," October 23, 1998. www.freedomforum.org.

Associated Press, "Jury set to decide if anti-abortion Web site, posters are protected speech," January 27, 1999. www.freedomforum.org.

Associated Press, "Oliver Stone ordered to give deposition in civil suit," March 29, 1999. www.freedomforum.org.

Associated Press, "San Diego parent asks county to pull gang memoir from school libraries," January 29, 1999. www.freedomforum.org.

Associated Press, "Supreme Court allows lawsuit against *Hit Man* publisher," April 20, 1998. www.freedomforum.org.

Associated Press, "Supreme Court won't free filmmaker from lawsuit over pair's crime spree," March 8, 1999. www.freedomforum.org.

Associated Press, "12-year-old's plea prompts school board to put book back on shelves," January 13, 1999. www.freedomforum.org.

Joan Biskupic, "High Court Expands Car Search Authority," *Washington Post*, April 6, 1999.

Joan Biskupic, "High Court Rejects Curbs on Ballot Initiatives," *Washington Post*, January 13, 1999.

Joan Biskupic, "High Court to Review Reporter Ride-Alongs in Police Raids," *Washington Post*, March 21, 1999.

Joan Biskupic, "Justice Blackmun Dies, Leaving Rights Legacy," *Washington Post*, March 5, 1999.

Joan Biskupic, "Justices Air Reservations About Anti-Loitering Ordinance," *Washington Post*, December 10, 1998.

Joan Biskupic, "Justices Question TV's Use on Raids," *Washington Post*, March 25, 1999.

Joan Biskupic, "Unanimous Decision Points to Tradition of Valuing Life," *Washington Post*, June 27, 1997.

Corey Q. Bradley, "Controversial speaker vows to defy any attempt to block Million Youth March," *Free!*, August 12, 1998.

Bill Broadway, "Court Ruling Highlights a Burden of Faith," *Washington Post*, July 5, 1997.

William Claiborne, "'Death with Dignity' Fight May Make Oregon National Battleground," *Washington Post*, June 27, 1997.

Don Colburn, "Another Chapter in the Case of Nancy Cruzan," *Washington Post*, October 16, 1990.

Malcolm Gladwell, "Woman in Right-to-Die Case Succumbs," *Washington Post*, December 27, 1990.

Susan B. Glasser, "Court's Ruling in Colorado Case May Reshape Campaign Finance," *Washington Post*, March 28, 1999.

Amy Goldstein, "High Court's Decision on Suicides Leaves Doctors in a Gray Zone," *Washington Post*, June 27, 1997.

Avram Goldstein, "Faith and Medicare Funding: Payments to Christian Science Nursing Centers Under Attack," *Washington Post*, March 22, 1999.

Linda Greenhouse, "Liberty to Reject Life," *New York Times*, June 27, 1990.

Richard S. Hoffman and Paul B. Gaffney, "Dealing with the Resurgent Prior Restraint," *Communications Lawyer*, Fall 1996.

David Hudson, "Appeals court lets decision stand in *Hit Man* case," *Free!*, December 17, 1997.

David Hudson, "Movie producers take First Amendment case to Louisiana high court," *Free!*, July 8, 1998.

Jeremy Leaming, "Appeals court: Despite religious objections, children must testify against father," *Free!*, April 12, 1999. www.freedomforum.org.

Jeremy Leaming, "Groups call on states to dump exemptions for faith-healing parents," *Free!*, June 12, 1998. www.freedomforum.org.

Jeremy Leaming, "Oregon lawmakers to reconsider regulations that protect faith-healing parents," *Free!*, January 27, 1999. www.freedomforum.org.

Jeremy Leaming, "Restoration drama: Downfall of federal religious-protection law produces new coalition strategy," *Free!*, April 9, 1998. www.freedomforum.org.

Jeremy Leaming, "Vouchers remain contentious issue in debate over government aid to religion," First Amendment Center, October 21, 1998. www.freedomforum.org.

Legal Times, "Final Frontier: Life, Death, and Law," November 13, 1989.

Andrew H. Malcolm, "Missouri Family Renews Battle Over Right to Die," *New York Times*, November 2, 1990.

Brooke A. Masters and David Nakamura, "Library's Internet Filtering Is Barred," *Washington Post*, November 24, 1998.

Tony Mauro, "Chicago's anti-gang law to face Supreme Court scrutiny," *Free!*, April 21, 1998. www.freedomforum.org.

Tony Mauro, "Supreme Court throws out Colorado's ballot-initiative rules," *Free!*, January 13, 1999. www.freedomforum.org.

Paul McMasters, "Books and movies as natural born killers," *Free!*, October 26, 1998. www.freedomforum.org.

Paul McMasters, "Nuremberg Files anti-abortion site: Free speech or hit list?" *Free!*, January 19, 1999. www.freedomforum.org.

Rene Sanchez, "Abortion Foes' Internet Site on Trial," *Washington Post*, January 15, 1999.

Rene Sanchez, "Doctors Win Suit over Antiabortion Web Site," *Washington Post*, February 3, 1999.

John Schwartz, "U.S. Judge Blocks Law Curbing Online Smut," *Washington Post*, February 2, 1999, p. A2.

Roberto Suro, "States to Become Forum for Fight over Assisted Suicide," *Washington Post*, June 27, 1997.

Phillip Taylor, "Congressional subcommittees schedule votes on flag amendment," *Free!*, April 12, 1999. www.freedomforum.org.

Washington Post, "Antiabortion Web Site Sued," January 8, 1999.

Internet

"ACLU v. Reno, Round 2: Broad Coalition Files Challenge to New Federal Net Censorship Law," Electronic Frontier Foundation Press Release, October 22, 1998. www.eff.org.

American Civil Liberties Union Home Page. www.aclu.org.

American Civil Liberties Union Briefing Paper Number 1, *Guardian of Liberty: American Civil Liberties Union*, 1997. www.aclu.org.

American Civil Liberties Union Briefing Paper Number 10, *Feedom of Expression*, 1997. www.aclu.org.

Campaign Finance series 1998. www.washingtonpost.com and www.Newsweek.com.

Children's Healthcare Is a Legal Duty (CHILD), *Data on religion-based medical neglect* and *Religious exemptions from healthcare for children*. www.childrenshealthcare.org.

Choice in Dying Home Page. www.echonyc.com.

The Communitarian Network, *The Responsive Communitarian Platform: Rights and Responsibilities*. www.gwu.edu/~ccps/RCPlatform.html.

"The Cosby Extortion Case," *Court TV Online*, December 12, 1997. www.courttv.com.

Electronic Frontier Foundation Home Page. www.eff.org.

Electronic Privacy Information Center Home Page. www.epic.org.

FindLaw Internet Legal Resources Home Page. www.findlaw.com.

"Florida Citizens File Lawsuit Against Unconstitutional 'Bible History' Classes," American Civil Liberties Union Press Release, December 9, 1997. www.aclu.org.

Free! The Freedom Forum Online. www.freedomforum.org.

Institute for Justice Home Page. www.ij.org.

"Many Companies Fail to Protect Confidential Employee Data," Electronic Privacy Information Center Press Release, April 22, 1996. www.epic.org/privacy/workplace/linowesPR.html.

Memorandum for the U.S. Secretary of Education and the U.S. Attorney General from William J. Clinton, July 12, 1995, quoted in *First Amendment Cyber-Tribune.* www.trip.com/FACT/1st.pres.rel.html.

"Mississippi Mother Wins School Prayer Challenge Before U.S. Judge," American Civil Liberties Union Press Release, June 3, 1996. www.aclu.org.

"National Sobriety Checkpoint Week," Mothers Against Drunk Driving (MADD) Public Policy Paper. www.madd.org.

People for the American Way Home Page. www.pfaw.org.

Privacy Rights Clearinghouse, *Fact Sheet #7: Is There Privacy in the Workplace?* www.privacyrights.org.

Privacy Rights Clearinghouse, *Fact Sheet #8: How Private Is My Medical Information?* www.privacyrights.org.

Reporters Committee for Freedom of the Press Home Page. www.rcfp.org.

Reporters Committee for Freedom of the Press, *The Privacy Paradox: Court Access.* www.rcfp.org.

Statement of Harvey Grossman, Legal Director, ACLU of Illinois, ACLU Supreme Court Preview: 1998 Term, *City of Chicago v. Jesus Morales, et al*, ACLU Press Release, October 1, 1998. www.aclu.org.

"Supreme Court Rules: Cyberspace Will Be Free!" American Civil Liberties Union Press Release, June 26, 1997. www.aclu.org.

Testimony of Solange E. Bitol, Legislative Counsel, American Civil Liberties Union, Washington National Office, Before the Senate Commerce, Science and Transportation Committee Hearing on Obscene Music Lyrics and the Effectiveness of Advisory Labels, June 16, 1998. www.aclu.org.

"Wisconsin Supreme Court Upholds School Vouchers, Victory for Parents, Institute for Justice," Institute for Justice Press Release, June 10, 1998. www.ij.org.

Index

abortion
  activism against, 16–17, 23–25
  attempts to regulate, 71–72
  right to, 68–70
Adventures of Huckleberry Finn (Twain), 44
Alderman, Ellen, 21
American Academy of Pediatrics, 54
American Civil Liberties Union (ACLU), 14, 90
American Library Association, 44, 90
American Psychological Association, 39
Amish, 53

Basketball Diaries, The (film), 38
Biggers, Neal B., 19
Bill of Rights, 7–8, 83
  liberties guaranteed in, 10
  new challenges to, 8–9
  right to privacy in, 67–68
  states must observe, 11–12
  see also civil liberties; First Amendment
Black, Hugo, 68
Black College Reunion, 32
Boerne v. Flores, 58
books
  inciting violence, 40–41
  limiting access to, 43–44
Brandeis, Louis D., 10
Brandenberg v. Ohio, 23, 25, 39–40
Brennan, William, 49, 68
Bryan, William Jennings, 61
Buckley v. Valeo, 29
Burger, Warren, 53

campaign spending, 29–30
Chaplinsky v. New Hampshire, 23

Chicago v. Morales, 34–36
Child Online Protection Act, 41, 43
children
  Internet access by, 41
  limiting book access to, 43–44
  medical treatment for, 54–55
  sexually explicit materials sold to, 42–43
Children's Healthcare Is a Legal Duty (CHILD), 54
Chopko, Mark E., 57
Christian Coalition, 56–57
Christian Scientists, 54–55
Church of Marijuana, 57
civil liberties
  common threads in, 12
  conflicting, 16–19
  court interpretations on, 15
  definition of, 6
  freedoms protected through, 10
  individual responsibilities and, 15–16
  interest groups supporting, 14
  legislation safeguarding, 14–15
  new challenges to, 8–9
  protecting, 82–83
  see also freedom of the press; freedom of speech; media; religious freedom; right to die
"clear and present danger" doctrine, 23
Clinton, Bill, 18
Columbine High School, 37–38
Communications Decency Act, 41
Communitarian Network, 16
Constitution, U.S.
  attempt to amend, 66
  civil liberties in, 6–7
  right to privacy in, 67–68

see also Bill of Rights
Corneal, Michael, 38
Cosby, Bill, 48
courts
  on disclosing personal information, 81
  on intrusive press coverage, 51
  press coverage in, 47–48
  on privacy law, 50
  see also U.S. Supreme Court
creationism, 62
Cruzan, Nancy, 73–76
Cruzan v. Director of Missouri Department of Health, 75

Daddy's Roommate (book), 44
Darrow, Clarence, 61
Dautrich, Kenneth, 28
Daytona Beach, Florida, 32
defamation. *See* libel law
demonstrations, 30–32
  antiabortion, 16–17
  antigay, 17–18
  restricting, 32–33
  see also freedom of assembly; public forums
doctors, violence against, 24
Douglas, William O., 33–34, 68
drug testing, 80

Employment Division v. Smith, 55–56
Epperson, Susan, 61–62
Equal Access Act of 1984, 14
Establishment Clause, 18, 52
  on church state separation, 58–59
  on privacy in government buildings, 64
  school prayer and, 60
  school voucher programs and, 63, 64
  teaching evolution and, 62
euthanasia, 73–76
evolution, taught in schools, 61–63

faith-healing, 53–55
Faith Tabernacle, 55
Federal Election Campaign Act, 29–30
Ferrea, Christopher, 24

Fifteenth Amendment, 11–12
films, 38, 41
First Amendment, 10–11
  free speech protection in, 20
  on hate speech, 25, 27–28
  Internet access and, 13–14
  libel law and, 49
  political speech and, 29
  pornography and, 42
  the press in, 45
  on religious liberty, 52
  on symbolic expression, 28, 29
  on use of force, 23
  see also Establishment Clause; Free Exercise Clause
Fiss, Owen, 22
flag burning, 28–29
Flag Protection Act of 1989, 28
Followers of Christ Church, 54
Fourteenth Amendment, 11–12
Fourth Amendment, 78
Free! (online publication), 58
freedom of assembly, 30–32
  gang loitering and, 33–36
  restricting, 32–33
  see also demonstrations; public forums
freedom of speech, 8, 20
  challenges established truths, 21–22
  famous defense of, 20–21
  hate speech and, 25–26
  Internet access and, 13–14
  marketplace theory of, 22
  public forums and, 26–28
  through campaign spending, 29–30
  through symbolic expression, 28–29
  violence incited by, 22–25
freedom of the press, 44–46
  in courtrooms, 47–48
  government secrets and, 46–47
  vs. privacy, 50–51
  protection from libel suits and, 48–50
  see also media
Free Exercise Clause, 18, 52, 53, 58
  limitations of, 55, 56
  school prayer and, 60, 61
  on scientific creationism, 62–63

gang loitering, 33–36
gays. *See* homosexuality
Giuliani, Rudolph, 33
Globe (tabloid), 49–50
Goosebumps (Stine), 44
government
  aid to religious schools, 63–64
  drug testing by, 80
  freedom stifled by, 7
  limited intervention by, 6, 12
  restricting religious practices, 56–57
  right to abortion and, 69
  searches by, 78–79
  separation from church, 52, 53, 59
Grossman, Harvey, 34

Hansen, Sandi, 24
Harlem, New York City, 33
Harris, Eric, 37–38
hate speech, 22, 25–26
health insurance industry, 81, 82
Heather Has Two Mommies (book), 44
Herdahl, Jason, 18–19
Hit Man: A Technical Manual for Independent Contractors (book), 40–41
Hoffman, Richard S., 51
Holmes, Oliver Wendell, 20, 21, 23
homosexuality
  activism against, 17–18
  in books, 44
Horsley, Neal, 24

I Know Why the Caged Bird Sings, (Angelou), 44
Inside Edition (TV program), 50
Institute for Justice, 14
Internet, 8
  antiabortion activism on, 23–24
  "blocking software" for, 13–14
  sex on, 41
interracial marriages, 68
It's Perfectly Normal (Harris), 44

Kaplan, Lewis, 33
Kennedy, Caroline, 21
King, Martin Luther, Jr., 49

Klebold, Dylan, 37–38
Ku Klux Klan, 21, 23

Lee v. Weisman, 60
legislation
  attempting to overthrow U.S. Supreme Court rulings, 65–66
  on faith-healing, 54
  on Internet access, 41
  on offensive media, 37
  protecting civil liberties, 14
  on public assembling, 33, 34
  regulating abortion, 71, 72
  on religious practices, 55, 56–58
  on teaching evolution, 62–63
Lemon test, 59
Lemon v. Kurtzman, 59
libel law, 48–50
liberty, 9
  see also civil liberties
libraries
  "blocking software" in, 13–14
  books removed from, 43–44
Lincoln, Abraham, 9
Linowes, David, 82
Littleton, Colorado, 37–38
loitering, gang, 33–36
Loudon Library Board, 13–14

Madison, James, 8, 66
marijuana, 57
Matsch, Richard, 47–48
McMasters, Paul, 25
media
  limitations on, 39–40
  limiting book access and, 43–44
  obscenity in, 42–43
  sex in, 41–42
  violence incited by, 37–39
  see also freedom of the press
Medical Information Bureau (MIB), 81
medical privacy, 80–82
medical treatment
  end-of-life decisions and, 72–73
  right to privacy and, 72–73
  vs. faith healing, 53–55
  see also right to die

Million Youth March, 32–33
Milwaukee Parental Choice Program, 64
"Monkey Trial," 61
Mortal Kombat (video game), 38
Muhammad, Khallid Abdul, 32–33

National Enquirer (tabloid), 49–50
National Governors Association, 36
"national security exception," 47
Native American Church, 55–56
Natural Born Killers (film), 41
Nazis, 27
New Republic (magazine), 57
newspapers. *See* freedom of the press
New York Times, 49
New York Times v. Sullivan, 49
New York Times v. United States, 46
Nixon, Shannon, 55
Nuremberg Files, 23–25

obscenity, 42–43
O'Connor, Sandra Day, 71, 78
Oklahoma City bombing, 47–48
On Scene: Emergency Response (TV program), 51
Osbourne, Ozzy, 38–39, 40

Pahl, Eileen, 34
Paladin Press, 41
Pentagon Papers, 46, 47
People for the American Way, 14, 56–57
peyote, 55–56
physician-assisted suicide, 76–78
Planned Parenthood, 24
Planned Parenthood v. American Coalition of Life Activists, 24
Planned Parenthood v. Casey, 71–72
political speech, 29–30
pornography, 22, 42
   see also obscenity
Portland Feminist Women's Health Center, 24
Posner, Richard, 51
prisoners
   religious freedom of, 57
Privacy Act of 1974, 14

privacy law, 50
   see also right to privacy
private schools, vouchers for, 63–64
public forums, 26–28
   see also demonstrations; freedom of assembly

rallies, 32–33
   see also demonstrations
Reed, Lowell A., 41–42
Rehnquist, William
   on abortion, 70
   on assisted suicide, 77
   on creation science, 63
religious freedom, 52–53
   efforts to change, 65–66
   faith-healing and, 53–55
   in government buildings, 64–65
   government limitations and, 58–59
   legislation permitting, 56–58
   peyote use and, 55–56
   school prayer and, 18–19, 59–61
   school voucher programs and, 63–64
   teaching theory of evolution and, 61–63
Religious Freedom Restoration Act of 1993, 56–58
reporters, 51
   see also freedom of the press
rights vs. responsibilities, 15–16
right to die, 73–76
   assisted suicide and, 76–78
right to privacy, 8, 10, 67–68
   abortion and, 69–70, 71
   disclosing personal information and, 80–83
   drug testing and, 80
   end-of-life decisions and, 72–73
   euthanasia and, 73–76
   government searches and, 78–79
   traffic checkpoints and, 79–80
Roe v. Wade, 69–70, 71
Rutherford Institute, 14

Scalia, Antonin
   on creation science, 63
   on peyote use, 55–56
schools

evolution taught in, 61–63
prayer in, 59–61
religion in, 18–19
voucher program for private, 63–64
scientific creationism, 62
Scopes, John T., 61
searches, government, 78–79
Sekulow, Jay, 17
sex
on the Internet, 41–42
see also obscenity; pornography
Skinner v. Railway Labor Executives' Association, 80
Skokie, Illinois, 27
slavery, 21–22
Society for the Right to Die, 76
Sowell, Thomas, 44
states
on abortion, 69, 72
bill of rights in, 7
must observe Bill of Rights, 11–12
religious freedom and, 58
Steinmetz, Donald, 64
Stevens, John Paul, 34–35
Stewart, Potter, 46
"Suicide Solution" (song), 38–39
Sullivan, L.B., 49
Supreme Court. *See* U.S. Supreme Court
Supreme Court of Wisconsin, 64
Swan, Rita, 54
symbolic expression, 28–29

television
intrusiveness in, 51
violence on, 39
see also freedom of the press; media
Tennessee v. Scopes, 61
Texas v. Johnson, 28
Thirteenth Amendment, 11–12
Thomas, Clarence, 35–36
Tinker v. Des Moines Independent Community School District, 28
traffic checkpoints, 79–80

U.S. Conference of Mayors, 36
U.S. Court of Appeals for the Fifth Circuit, 61

U.S. Supreme Court, 15
on abortion, 69, 71–72
on antiabortion activism, 16–17
on assisted suicide, 76–77
on campaign spending, 29–30
on "clear and present danger" doctrine, 23
on disclosing personal information, 80–81
on drug testing, 80
efforts to overthrow rulings of, 65–66
on faith-healing, 55
on flag burning, 28–29
on freedom of assembly, 31–32, 33–34
on freedom of speech, 22
on freedom of the press, 46–47
on gang loitering, 34–36
on hate speech, 25, 27
on libel law, 48, 49
on media violence, 39–49, 41–42
on news vs. entertainment, 51
on obscenity, 42
on pornography, 42
on privacy from government, 79
on religious freedom, 53, 58–59
on right to die, 75
on right to privacy, 67–68
on school prayer, 18, 59–60
on school voucher programs, 64
on sex on the Internet, 41
on teaching evolution, 62
on traffic checkpoints, 79–80
on use of peyote, 55–56
see also courts

violence
incited by free speech, 22–25
media incites, 38–39
through antiabortion activism, 23–25
voucher programs, 63–64

Washington Post, 46
Weber, Walter, 58
West Paducah, Kentucky, 38

Picture Credits

Cover photo: © Dennis Brack/Black Star
Archive Photos, 11
Archive Photos/Chris Smith, 48
FPG International, 9, 26, 35, 65, 70, 72, 80
Jeff Greenberg/Archive Photos, 53, 57
Library of Congress, 7, 13, 15
Ken Love/Archive Photos, 27
PhotoDisc, 76
Reuters/Grigory Dukor/Archive Photos, 31
Reuters/Stephen Jaffe/Archive Photos, 45
Reuters/Eric Miller/Archive Photos, 17
Reuters/Jeff Mitchell/Archive Photos, 38
University of Minnesota, 62
Who Photo/PH. Wolmuth, 21

About the Author

Debbie Levy writes nonfiction, fiction, and poetry for adults and children. Her work on topics ranging from law to parenting to cyberspace has appeared in books, as well as in such publications as the *Washington Post*, *Legal Times*, *Washington Parent*, and *Highlights for Children*. Before turning to her writing career, Ms. Levy practiced law with a large Washington, D.C., law firm, and served as editor for a national chain of newspapers for lawyers. She earned a B.A. in government and foreign affairs from the University of Virginia, and a J.D. and M.A. in politics from the University of Michigan. Ms. Levy enjoys kayaking and fishing in the Chesapeake Bay region, hiking just about anywhere, and playing the piano. She lives with her husband and their two sons in Chevy Chase, Maryland.

Bethany Christian
High School Library
Goshen, Indiana